ERODE

SONS OF GODS MC

ELIZABETH KNOX

CONTENTS

WARNING

This content is intended for
mature audiences only.

It contains material that may be viewed as offensive to some
readers, including graphic language, dangerous and sexual
situations, and extreme violence.

PROLOGUE

PAN

3 months earlier . . .

We just came back to the club. Some of us came from the hospital, and the rest of us from seeing that the few straggling fucks from the Vile Serpents were disposed of.

Many of us have been holding a vigil ever since we got Zeus in through the emergency room doors. It's been utter fucking chaos since the very moment that Thorn and the Vile Serpents walked into *Shots* with guns in hand. I always knew Thorn was bad news, and watching the way he had been treating Calli, made me uneasy. I just never expected him to be that damn bold.

A blatant attack on an innocent party of people that weren't all club members in the middle of a public place—a place that's supposed to be neutral territory—it's just unheard of. It goes against the unwritten code we all follow.

I guess Thorn really showed his true colors here. He doesn't give a flying fuck about codes, decency, or honor. He only cares about himself, and it's never been more evident than it is right now.

Hades is acting as interim Prez right now, and he's barreling through the club. I know he's already spoken with Eros, who's beside himself, about the shape Calli's in. He stayed behind at the hospital to care for her rather than come check on her father.

I know whatever Hades said, it was to ease both her mind and his, so the two could rest, and she could begin her healing.

The doc had to be called out to do an exam on her already while Hades and a few of us were gone to check in on Zeus. We had to make sure he didn't kick the fuckin' bucket while we were rescuing Calli.

I'm sure Hades will call church soon to see what we can do to get back at those fuckers, but for now, it's a waiting game to get the information we need to get back at Thorn.

I don't know what the hell I would do if it was my ol' lady who had been taken, especially in such a violent way.

I know Eros is probably blaming himself on the inside. He's being really strong for everyone, for her, but I know that he can break at any moment. Hell, I would've broken already if I were him. That's what I like about him. He's as strong as hell.

I look like it on the outside, but I'm just not. I like to fuck around with women, as wild as they come, and I can laugh the loudest. But you know what they say about those who laugh the loudest.

Inside, I'm carrying a lot of weight, and a lot of hatred, that no one would ever know looking at me.

I follow Hades into the office and face his rage head-on. I know he's got some shit on his mind, and I know he's going to need us to be there for him more than ever. He may be a very capable VP and interim Prez, but on top of dealing with the fact that Zeus is in the hospital injured and everyone trying to find Calli these past few days, I'm sure he's spread pretty damn thin.

"Put me to work. How can I help? I can't just sit by and watch Eros and Calli lose it like that.

Hades isn't like Zeus. He doesn't hesitate. He doesn't need to judge my character or my well-being at the moment. "I know I didn't say a whole lot at the hospital when they told me what was up. It's because I don't know what to say, and I don't want to start a panic."

Hades has those dark circles under his eyes and considering he's tried to get an update on Zeus and be by his side as much as possible while also running the club, he likely hasn't slept much at all, if any.

I grab the chair in front of me, hanging onto it for dear life.

We all saw him go down. He was shot in the chest. Honestly, I didn't know that he'd even make it to the damn hospital. But it's been days now, and he ain't dead. That has to give us some kind of hope, so I breathe a sigh of relief and let Hades tell me. "How bad is it really? Are we looking at losing our Prez?"

I try to keep my voice down, knowing that no one needs to hear that shit right now, especially because morale will be low. And who the hell knows if Thorn is gonna try to pull some even worse shit. Show up at the clubhouse guns blazing or something. I know a lot of the prospects in the clubhouse are gonna feel like nowhere is safe.

And Gemma is just hysterical.

He slams his fists onto the desk, a new crack appearing in it. Fuck. It's gotta be bad for Hades to be reacting this way. "He's doing pretty damn well, considering."

I shake my head and wait for him to meet my eyes. "That's not an answer."

"The docs say it's a miracle he made it this far. Telling Calli that, well, I don't think it's a good idea right now. She needs to focus on herself. There's a hell of a lot of trauma that's gonna come up from what just happened, not to mention the physical."

He shakes his head in disgust, and I find myself gripping the chair even harder. My fingers are going numb from the pressure. I can only imagine what actually happened to her, but by the way she looks, I know it was bad.

Yet, another thing I didn't think the Vile Serpents were capable of.

We've always known that they were shitty. Selling drugs to minors was one of the things that we became aware of, but I never would've guessed that Thorn was going as far as to actually harm innocent women like this. Just because he didn't get his fucking way.

"I kind of get it, but we can't keep the truth from them forever, especially if he's not doing well. Calli will want to say goodbye if it goes south."

Hades looks up, his eyes furious. "You shut the fuck up about that shit. We can't think like that. Zeus can't go anywhere. He just finally saw his daughter for the first time in years. I'm not going to accept that as a possibility. Besides, like we all said, it's a miracle. Hopefully, the miracle holds out, considering he survived the initial bullet. Which is amazing since it hit him right in the chest."

I nod. "Okay, fine. That's fair. But keeping secrets for too long can be devastating. What about Eros? He at least should know in case he needs to tell her, right? "

Hades stares blankly at me, and I glean the truth. "You're shitting me, right? Eros doesn't even know?"

"Look, I don't want anything to come between Eros and his ol' lady. Especially right now. The thing is, if he has to lie to her to make sure that she focuses on herself, then what's that going to do if she finds out? It's gonna tear away at their relationship and ruin it. Which none of us needs right now. Zeus has already given his blessing to them. The best thing for Calli is that all of us keep our fucking mouths shut, do you understand me?"

I know not to dick around with Hades. If there's anyone in the club as scary as Zeus could be on his worst days, it's Hades. Half the time, if Hades is around, we don't even need a damn enforcer. Hades just has to look the asshole in the eye, and they go tuck their tail and run.

I survey Hades for a moment, his hard exterior, and wonder why he even gives a shit about stuff like this anyway. I wouldn't take him for someone who would. Hell, why does it matter to him if Eros and Calli stay together?

But then I start thinking about myself. There are things that people don't realize or notice about me. The real me. Maybe there's been someone down the line who was lost to him because he lied to them. Friend, family member, lover, doesn't matter. That kind of shit sticks with you, and you learn your lesson. Otherwise, you live a life full of heartbreak because you're fucking alone.

I don't press it, though. If he ever wants to tell anybody what the hell actually went down in his personal life, he can, and he will. Neither of us is here for that right now.

"Do you have anything I can do? Other than keep a damn secret?" I ask him, my frustration making my nerves jittery.

"I need you to keep this shit on the low down, you got it?"

Whatever it is, it must be damn good.

"I need you to go out and look for traces of the Vile Serpents MC."

"The Vile Serpents? Don't we already fucking know where their base is at? Where do they hang out? If that's what you want, why don't we just ambush them?"

Hades crosses his arms over his chest. "Just got word as we were coming back to the club that intel says they've left the area entirely. Said Thorn gathered everyone up and ran. I know better, though."

This can't be good. A whole MC just disappearing. Sounds like the calm before the storm.

"It's complete bullshit to think that Thorn would ever leave this place. They'll be around somewhere, but probably not at their clubhouse. They know that they violated pretty much every code we have. When word of what he and his club did gets around, it won't be just us that's pissed off at them," Hades continues.

I smile at that thought. Damn, I'd love that war to go to Thorn's doorstep with three or four, even five MCs, all right there to put a bullet in his head as well as every single Vile Serpent who doesn't immediately surrender.

"Yeah, I'll do my best. I won't tell Eros anything about Zeus for now."

Hades looks satisfied with my response and lets me go. I immediately head back out but then stop dead in my tracks down the hall. I lock eyes with Trix, who's in the hallway, leaning against the wall.

Damn, she should've gone home, but I know she and Gemma are begging for updates about Calli, trying to be there for her. Trix was beside herself and couldn't let it go.

What has she heard, though? She could easily be the one to blow the information about Zeus to Calli.

No, I doubt she heard anything. She probably has just been pacing around aimlessly. I wave at her as I go by and then go outside to get on my bike.

Hades just trusted me with a big job. Probably one of the biggest jobs I've ever done.

I'm going to scour every place in Birmingham and the surrounding areas to make sure I don't let the MC down. I'm going to find these assholes so we can bring them to justice for what they did to us, even if it's the last thing I do.

CHAPTER ONE

Present Day . . .

It's a quiet day at the house, which is nice after all the chaos that's been going on in our lives. Calli has been able to go back to work at *Shots* since her kidnapping, though the club never leaves her alone. There's always someone watching her. Whether it's Eros' orders or straight from Zeus, I don't know. But I'm so glad she's all right.

And I don't just mean physically. I know what happened to her now. It's taken her months to tell us all, and I know how that kind of trauma can really fuck a girl up.

I turn the pages of the book I'm reading. It's not something I do too often, but Pearl loaned me one of her books. I wanted to see what the hype was all about, so I took her up on the challenge.

Man, now I know why she holes up in her room with these pages all the time. Some of these men and sexy scenes . . . well, they go well with a little Netflix and chill all by my damn self. Who needs a real man that can lie and cheat when they have a book boyfriend who does it so well without all the real drama?

I laugh at a joke on the page when I sit straight up in bed.

The sound of the keys in the door brings me out of my room to see who it is. It's a few minutes after four in the afternoon. I wasn't expecting anyone but Pearl in her room, as usual, to be here for a couple more hours.

Both Calli and Gemma are supposed to be at work. But when I walk into the room, I see Gemma throwing down her keys and stomping in her boots toward our bathroom. "I thought you had to work 'til six." I follow her to find out what's brought her home early.

She loves her job most days, but her boss is a high-strung dragon lady who needs constant attention. Gemma getting off early is unheard of unless it's a special occasion or emergency.

"I asked to get off early. I got some news." I watch as she becomes like a tornado, going through the house and picking up all the things she needs. A hairbrush, a dress, some boots. Filling her purse with little odds and ends.

She doesn't look like it, but she's one of those women who is always prepared for anything. She even keeps a first aid kit in her jacked-up truck, especially now that we had all lived through what we did at *Shots*. Not that a first aid kit is going to save anyone from a bullet to the chest, but it makes her feel better, so that's what matters.

In a matter of minutes, she has slipped on a slinky dress, bodycon, and is pulling it up at the sides, in a mauve color. She wears knee-high, velvet black boots with stiletto heels. Her hair has been brushed out wild around her head like a fairy.

I envy the way she does that sometimes, pulling herself together so quickly and so easily. I spend hours on my makeup.

"Where the hell are you going?" I ask her, seeing she's in a hurry but also dressed to the nines.

"To the clubhouse, of course. You're coming with me, right?" she asks.

I look down at my black, high water skinny jeans and my black crop top, my hair up in a messy bun. At least my makeup is done. I pretty much never do anything, even lounge around the house, without doing my makeup. There's just something I love about it. It makes me feel put together even on days when I feel a mess internally.

I pull the flannel over my ensemble from the back of the couch and reach for my favorite pair of shoes with a shrug. "Sure. What's going on there? Is Zeus finally back?"

"I got a phone call that Zeus is coming home today. Let's load your cupcakes in the back of the truck."

I've been prepping for the possibility for two days now, knowing Calli would want to celebrate. I love baking, so I figure I might as well put that to good use.

"So, he's gonna be okay, then?" I ask, remembering the uncertainty over the past few weeks. The ups and downs and tears Calli would spill alone in her room and pretend we couldn't hear her.

"Yeah. He had to have a couple of surgeries, and you know there have been complications, but they finally feel he's pulled through enough to come back out. I figured we could go welcome him home and celebrate. Be there for Calli and all too." Gemma fumbles with one of her earrings while stomping over to Pearl's door and knocking on it. "Hey, girl, we're going to the clubhouse. Zeus is coming home. You coming with us?"

Pearl hollers from behind the door, "I'll be around later."

Gemma scoops her keys back up, and I follow her out the door, cupcakes in hand, to slide them into the backseat alongside the ones in Gemma's arms. I climb up into the passenger seat of her jacked-up 1975 Ford pickup. This baby blue monster, as I sometimes call it, still runs like it's brand new.

One of the many things that Pan did for Gemma was making sure that she had a good mechanic for this thing, period. Otherwise, it would never survive. And it's the most reliable car that any of us has. Gemma's always the one to call when we have car trouble or something.

Plus, the damn thing is a tank. It isn't like it could ever be destroyed in a crash.

She revs the engine, and it rumbles to life, shaking beneath me. We pull out of the driveway, and Gemma's routine of gossip begins.

Something else about living with Gemma, everything is her damn business. I've gotten used to it over the years since knowing her, and I wouldn't have it any other way. It's just this one thing I really don't want to talk about. As far as I'm concerned, it's open and shut.

"You and Pan still having an issue?"

I shrug, pretending it was no big deal. Because honestly, he doesn't deserve for me to make it a big deal. "I don't give a fuck if Pan has an issue with me. He was the one talking so loud, and no one should've been lying to Calli about how her dad was actually doing. I don't care what they were trying to do to protect her or whatever bullshit reason they gave. She deserved to know. "

I look down at my French manicured nails, focusing on them rather than Gemma or the road, hoping the conversation will be over.

"I couldn't do it. Not the way you two looked at each other before. You've got balls of steel."

"I'm not a pussy. It's that simple." I look out the window, thinking about all of the lies I've been told throughout my life. I don't want to deal with any more liars. I don't care what the excuse is. I hate them more than I hate anything or anyone in the world, which is saying something.

I may look like some beautiful, bubbly, 20-something, but underneath is a whole world of darkness no one knows about or could begin to understand. I'm careful who I spend my time on and with, and generally, once my good opinion is lost, it's gone for good.

We pull up to the clubhouse, and a couple of the bikers are outside. I recognize one of them as Hermes, the one with the long, white beard and graying hair. The other has super long, brown hair, a black vest, and only a few tats. He is a pretty good-looking muscular guy, but I can't remember his name.

I spent quite a lot of time here after Calli was found, but I wasn't a regular like Gemma. Especially after Pan and I had a falling out, there didn't seem like much of a reason to be around.

Gemma reaches into the backseat to grab the cupcakes. They're pretty damn beautiful if I do say so myself. The icing is black and gold, and they have all assortments of decorations on them.

I grab my fair share and get out of the truck. As I hop down, the heels send shockwaves up my legs.

I notice as we get out that the MC men are watching Gemma in particular. Between what she's wearing, her wild, red hair, and the way she carries herself, I don't blame them. Gemma's one of those women who lights up a room when she walks into it. She always becomes the center of attention.

But as much as these men like women and sometimes inappropriate flirting, they never touch Gemma.

If Pan's around, I notice that they even try to avert their gazes entirely. She's like the forbidden apple, with Pan being her brother. I wonder if any of them will ever be brave enough to go after her.

I know some of them might be because she told me that she fucked one of them. Of course, I don't even know which one. They were both smart enough to keep it on the down-low after the fact. As much as she made a big deal about Pan and I maybe sleeping together at some point, Pan would've been a bigger problem if he found out she was with one of the MC guys.

I used to think it was sweet because he was protecting her. He didn't want his sister with one of these rough old men. He didn't want her involved in this life at all. But now, any good opinions of him have gone to shit. Who can fault me for hating liars, though?

As Gemma starts to walk by Hermes, he gives a long whistle. "You look fine as hell."

Well, I guess that answers my question, though I don't know if either of us could take him seriously since he's kind of like a big brother or old man and uncle, really.

He's always joking.

"Come on, you know I'm not into old guys. Though maybe you'll get lucky. Maybe one night I'll get drunk enough while I'm here to fuck you," Gemma responds, a sly grin on her face.

The younger guy next to him starts cracking up. I smile despite myself. Hermes hits the guy in the arm, hard. "Shut the hell up, Cronos." So, his name is Cronos, God of time, Titan. Interesting.

Gemma walks right past them and up the steps to the club-house doors, carrying the cupcakes with her. She walks like she owns the damn place, and not for the first time, I wish I had her air of confidence. Not that I have zero, I'm just not the take charge of a room type. I'm more the stand back and watch what's going on type.

Cronos hops in front of us right as we approach the door. He steps in front of Gemma, forcing her to almost drop the cupcakes. I watch the exchange and wonder if this is the guy she fucked because of the way he's looking at her. He opens up the plastic container and pulls out one of the cupcakes. I can see the frustration bubbling under the surface for Gemma. She may have come in a small package, but she has a temper just as hot as any of these men.

Cronos puts the cupcake up to his mouth, sticks his tongue out, and begins to lap up the icing in the most sexually provocative way possible. In fact, I'm about to offer myself to him from the display. "Anytime you want me to lick your cupcake, all you have to do is give me a call."

I don't know whether that was the cheesiest fucking pickup line I've ever seen and heard or if it was damn brilliant. Cronos reaches for Gemma's crossbody purse and opens it, rummaging through it as it dangles off her right shoulder, finally pulling out her cell phone.

Well, if anyone's going to get into Gemma's pants, it's this guy. He has balls bigger than the rest of these guys, for sure.

"What's your passcode?" he asks her.

Gemma tells him, and he puts his number in the phone before placing the phone back in her bag. I can't help but snicker at it as he moves aside, leaving us clear to walk in.

Pan greets us as my face goes blank. "What the hell did Cronos just do?" he asks Gemma

Pan was talking to his sister, but he was glaring at me. If ever I felt totally unwanted somewhere in my life, it's now. But I'm not here for him, so I don't give a shit. This is about Calli and her father. Celebrating that despite all of the worry and how bad off he was, and despite all the lies, he is coming home.

"It was nothing. You know how the guys are." Gemma squints a challenge at him, practically daring her brother to call her out on the lie. Instead, he turns to me.

"Why the hell are you even here? You don't even like the club."

I gulp at his statement, stepping forward just a little so I'm closer to his face. I want him to know that his intimidation tactics won't work on me. "It's not that I don't like the club. I don't like *you*."

Gemma starts laughing hysterically, the cupcake tin shaking around in her grasp. Pan's eyes go wide. "You're the *only* woman who doesn't like me. You know that?"

I roll my eyes. "I'm not a fan of liars and never will be." I step around him and walk toward the kitchen, Gemma following behind. I don't have time for his bullshit or patience. I'm worth more than that anyway.

CHAPTER TWO

Trix's been cold as fuckin' ice since the day I caught her in the hallway headed out to look for any signs of the Vile Serpents MC, and now, here she is in front of me. She's looking at me like I just killed somebody and calling me a liar.

I don't like her fucking tone or assumptions. I thought Trix was hot shit when I met her, and truthfully, she still is, but there's something dark and mean under there I'm not sure I bargained for. She has all these strong opinions, it seems. I thought it was aimed at the club in general, so I gave her space.

I mean, she witnessed a shootout, Zeus nearly dying in the process, and Calli getting kidnapped . . . it's a hell of a lot for all of us. And she's just a regular civilian. She didn't expect that to be going the fuck down at a birthday party.

I thought she was processing or just hating on the dangerous way of life.

I can handle that, but being called a liar?

I want to tell her right now how damn wrong she is. She doesn't get how the club fucking works. Even Gemma knows better. Yeah, right now, she's laughing like a damn bitch, but she does that to press my buttons. It's her fucking job.

Trixie doesn't have to be like this. If she would just listen.

But she walks away and leaves me hanging the same way she's done for three months now.

I give Gemma a hard look, and she shrugs while she carries the cupcakes toward the kitchen.

I seethe, wondering if I should just let it go. For some reason, though, the encounter really ruffles my feathers. I didn't choose to lie to Calli. I didn't lie at all. Luckily, she never directly asked me how Zeus was doing or if I heard anything new. She left it up to Eros to get her the news through Hades or another officer.

But even if she had asked and I told her the same shit Hades had, it wouldn't be my fault. Hades made the decision as acting Prez. It's not something I was going to risk questioning or even could question if I wanted to keep both my fucking balls intact as well as my membership.

I had to step in line to follow the orders. There was no other decision to make.

Gemma comes back a moment later, breaking me out of the thought pattern. "You look bothered, big bro," she says, flicking a piece of stray hair on my forehead. I glare down at her, crossing my arms over my body.

"That's because I *am* bothered. I'm sure as hell bothered by that. You know how this shit works now, Gemma. You've made it a fucking point to stick your nose in it now." Internally, I'm disgusted with myself. I feel like a dad, lecturing her like this rather than her helpful big brother. She's trying to look out for us both in her own way and not take sides.

"Look, I'm sorry, but I am bothered. I've gotta talk to her."

I walk away with Gemma warning me, "I don't think it's going to help you one bit right now."

I walk into the kitchen, immaculate thanks to the prospects and ready especially for today's occasion.

Zeus is coming home, and we're all damn glad about it. Not only because it means he finally made it out of the woods, but because Hades is becoming too damn much.

We're all grateful for the guy, but his intensity gets everyone on edge too easily.

Three lights shine down on the marble countertop, a fresh bouquet of white flowers in a vase at the center giving the room a sweet scent. Brand new bar stools sit at one end, and Trix is at the other, facing away from me.

She stands next to the sink, putting the cupcakes she brought on display on a tray on the counter below the small window in the room. She's meticulously sliding each one onto the platter so that they are an even width apart.

I don't know if she knows she's being watched and is avoiding any conversation with me or if she's just that OCD about it.

Everyone else is back out in the main area of the club, anxiously awaiting our fearless leader's return. It's as good a time as any to try and solve this the right way.

I take a deep breath and try to quell my anger about the situation. If she doesn't understand, that's cool. Trixie doesn't strike me as the rough and tumble type. She wouldn't know anything about this if it wasn't for her association with Gemma and myself. She'd probably never even run across a biker.

She's far too put together for that.

I shuffle my feet a little loudly as I walk further into the room and pull out one of the barstools so I can sit. Maybe it'll make me seem less threatening and more like an ally.

I honestly don't know why I'm trying so fucking hard or why her opinions bother me so damn much. Any other chick, I'd flip off and let the fuck go. There's something about Trix, though, that gets under my skin. In all the good ways and the bad.

Her stance shifts and she turns to the side to look at me before going back to playing with the cupcakes. "What else did you come to lie to me about?" she asks under her breath, and I clench my fists on the countertop. She's pressing every damn button I've got, and she knows it. I can't let her win at this game.

"Look, Trix, you don't understand how shit runs around here. I know it's not something you're used to or that I would expect you to, but . . ."

She turns around and cuts me off, her hooded eyes looking bored, which is somehow worse than anger. She sighs loudly at me and declares, "I just don't want to know, Pan."

My brows dip down toward my eyes, creases appearing on my forehead in confusion and anger. What the hell is wrong with her?

It's like she's judging me without knowing anything about me. Our conversations up 'til now have been surface level. Some flirting. Nothing fucking more than that, and they were pleasant at least. So, where does she get off making assumptions about the club or about me when she knows nothing more than the few incidents she's seen for the sake of her roommates?

And yeah, I'm sure Gemma's had a good time talking shit about me to her roommates. She's my sister, though, and Trix or anyone should know that a sibling's opinion is going to be tainted from years of sibling rivalry and having to grow up side-by-side.

She can't think the worst of me for no reason, especially when things I did or didn't do are being taken out of context.

"I'm going to tell you anyway because I'm not going to have you judging me like this. When you're part of an MC, you follow the rules."

I pause, looking at her to see if she's at all listening. She just stands there, so at least it's not combative anymore. "Whatever the Prez or officers say goes, and I answer to the club. No one else."

"I'm at least glad it's not God," Trix pops off, immediately turning to the side to pick at some icing on one of the cupcakes.

I stiffen at the comment. What the hell kind of response was that? Answering to God? Is that what she's talking about?

I didn't take her for a religious person, and I don't understand the reference. However, from the way her shoulders are slumped, as if in defeat, and how she won't even look at me now, I think her own word vomit has caught her by surprise too.

I watch her, and she's fucking rattled. There's something here I didn't see before.

It makes me wonder what's going on in that head of hers.

Suddenly, she whips back around, but now, she has her poker face on. One I only know because so many of the guys do the same damn thing when they need to shove their emotions deep down.

I put the idea in my back pocket of how she's hiding something, as well as the fact that Trix's mood can change on a dime. There's more to her than meets the eye. I suppose I judged her as well, but it doesn't make her assumptions okay.

Trix no longer looks rattled but now looks like she's ready to fight.

"Look, Trix, it's like a code. It's not just MCs that have it. Pirates, thieves, the Navy, fraternities, and the mafia, whether good or bad, there is a pledge you have to make when you join these things. The biggest thing, more than anything, is that when my Prez tells me to do something, I have to do it. I have no authority here, and for good reason. I'm a young inexperienced shithead compared to Zeus and Hades. They know how to keep this operation running and keep us all safe. That's what matters." My hands are going wild with gestures, trying to get her to understand. My passion for it may have gotten a little out of control here.

Trix scoffs and shakes her head. "Why do you even feel like you owe me an explanation?"

I stop, and she has a damn good point. Even if she's playing devil's advocate here, I don't owe her anything, especially an explanation. It just pisses me off that she won't listen to reason.

"I have to go handle some shit," I mutter after a moment spent in silence, racking my brain to come up with an answer. I'm not able to think of any other more graceful way out of the conversation. I have to get away from her before I lose my shit.

CHAPTER THREE

I finish eating my cupcake, desperately trying to clear my mind from what's weighing heavily on it. I don't know what it is about Pan that gets me so worked up when I'm around him. Sure, we had a little flirtatiousness for a bit there, and I thought something was going to happen, but it's not the end of the world that it didn't.

In fact, considering he decided to show his true colors to me with the way that he's such a slave to the MC that he'll lie to somebody that's close to him, it's probably best that nothing did happen between us. But for some reason, the fact that we keep fighting like this and the fact that he seems to go back and forth between hating me and trying to prove himself to me is just making my skin crawl. My nerves are on edge, and I can't say why. He's just another guy.

It's not like I don't know lots of guys. In fact, there are a shit ton of guys here today. I could bat my pretty eyes, show some of my body off, and probably get any of them that I wanted. That's not necessarily my style right now, but I could. So, what is it about this one?

The vibe is weird. It's giving me the bad kind of goosebumps all over, and I kind of wish I could just go take a shower and go back to bed right now. But I need to be here. Calli needs a united front for Zeus, and whether or not I'm in the MC, I'm her roommate and her friend. That makes me a part of this. I need to stop feeling like I should be answering to other people. I thought I'd learned my lesson on that. I've been through enough hell to know better.

I just need to shake it off.

I hear cheers and claps and know that it means that Zeus has arrived. I opt to stay in the kitchen, for now, knowing people will be coming in soon to grab these cupcakes anyway. They're not kidding when they talk about men's stomachs. Men love food, especially sweets. These men are going to devour these cupcakes even if they're shitty.

Shortly after the cheers die down, Gemma comes into the room. There's a beer in her hand. "Where'd you get the beer, Gemma?"

Gemma scrunches up her face and then giggles. "I snatched it from Hades when he wasn't looking. He was too busy playing pool. Plus, he pissed me off. You know how much I love that." She rolls her eyes, her words dripping in sarcasm.

And she thinks I'm brave? She's the ballbuster, and everyone knows it. I'm not around that much, but I know to be frightened of Hades. Not only is he the VP, but he has been interim Prez while Zeus has been away. Calli and Eros have come home with too many stories about his behavior and attitude, and he looks intimidating to boot. I certainly wouldn't fuck with him.

"I took it as a consolation prize for dealing with his ass." Gemma shrugs and takes a big swig.

The crash of pool balls against each other fills the silence and then comes the grumbling. "Where the hell did my drink go? Poseidon, what the fuck. Did you take my drink?" I meet Gemma's eyes, and we start to snicker. He seriously has no idea that Gemma is the one who took his drink even though she's the one who's no longer there.

That's when Calli walks into the room. I'm so glad to see that she's smiling. Her eyes narrow in on the beer in Gemma's hand. "I think I know exactly where it is," she calls back out toward the men playing pool, unable to keep a straight face. I giggle a little more, but Gemma is unable to control her laughter, so she quickly tries to shut it up with another swig of the beer she stole.

Gemma sets the beer down and then slides up onto the island because the chair, of course, is too boring for Gemma. "Yeah, well, Hades was being a dick so . . ."

Calli snorts and then covers her mouth in shock, causing all three of us to break out in full-blown laughter. I hold my stomach as the muscles clench painfully. It's nice that we've been able to get back to this. Things were real dark there for a little bit after Calli came back to us, and for absolutely good reason.

I liked her before, but I certainly have a newfound respect for her. She's been damn strong through this and mostly worried about her father. And I think him being back will transform her even more. I hope they get to form the relationship they deserve now that he's out of the woods.

Speak of the devil.

Zeus walks in pretending as if he was never shot in the chest in the first place. Surely, he's bandaged underneath his cut, but you wouldn't know it by the smirk on his face. He's trying very hard to wipe it off, but I suspect he's heard Gemma. "I'm guessing you heard what Gemma just said?"

Gemma grits her teeth in an awkward smile, trying to look innocent, but we both know that's not possible for her.

Zeus chuckles and says, "She's not wrong."

Gemma cackles. "Maybe I do like old guys." I look at Calli as she turns to Gemma and gives her an odd look, and then glares at her. I keep my mouth shut, knowing Gemma meant it as a joke, but obviously, Calli's sensitive about her dad right now. And for good reason.

It's Zeus who chills the air. He gestures by putting his hands across each other and then brings them out like a no-go. "I've got someone I'm keeping an eye on anyway." He pats Calli on the shoulder reassuringly.

Calli's head whips around to her father. I remember her mentioning a few times that her father had been fucking one of the clubwhores. She said how she and the woman didn't get along. In fact, he even had a baby with the clubwhore.

That's gotta be awkward, but Calli's face lights up, showing that she's much more interested in her father being with somebody else. Though, I do wonder about the dynamic between him and her mother now that the two of them have talked it out.

That's the one thing Calli hasn't talked much about since her mother is back to not communicating too much with her and trying to process everything. Or at least that's her excuse for not talking. Call it the trust issues talking, but I feel it runs deeper than that.

"Oh, like who?" Calli asks him. All of us lean in, waiting for his answer, intrigued by who the Prez would be so into.

"Unfortunately, someone who isn't giving me the time of day."

I turn to the side and cover my mouth, hiding my smile. Intuition tells me exactly who he means. He doesn't mean anybody in this clubhouse. He wants Calli's mother back. I haven't been around Zeus very much, but I can tell right away that he loves and cares for his family. I see it most in the way he treats Calli, even though he hasn't been around for most of her life. It's obvious he regrets it.

I'm sure he also regrets whatever went down between him and Calli's mother too.

Which is another reason why the way that Hades and Pan handled themselves about the information they were keeping from Calli is unacceptable to me. I don't think Zeus would've felt the same way. He would've wanted his daughter to know and be by his side.

I turn back around and clear my throat, changing the subject. "So, how does it feel to be back home?"

Zeus pats the spot lightly where he was shot. He winces a little, which tells me he's still in a bit of pain. "Look, anything is better than that stuffy hospital. I was so ready to be out of there and back with my daughter and in my own damn bed."

Calli shakes her head at his stubbornness and follows him, watching his every move nervously as he walks over to the cupcakes. I stand up straight, wondering what he's going to think of them.

I've never done much of anything with my talent other than bake for people I care about. That is until Gemma encouraged me to start my own business. It's nothing fancy, but I have a few clients, and I do it all out of the house. It pays the bills, but I always get so self-conscious about how people are going to receive my food the very first time, especially the guests of honor.

"Trix, you did a great job decorating these. They look like a real professional's work."

I blush and gesture to them. "I actually baked them all too. It's kind of a thing I do, especially when I'm on edge. Now, it gets to be my job too." I walk over to him as he picks one up.

Zeus takes a bite and smiles deviously. "It's so moist, just the way I like it." He winks at me.

Calli shivers, staring her father down. "I have never ever wanted to hear you say something like that. Please don't do it again." I can't help but laugh at that.

Gemma hops down from the island, holding her stomach as she goes into a fit of laughter.

"You know what, girls?" Zeus says as he's finishing the cupcake, "I'm going to make Sunday dinners a thing again. Trix, will you handle dessert for them? I mean, since you like it and you're so good at it."

I perk up a little. "Oh, yeah. I'd love to."

"Thanks, Trix. Now, I'm off to enjoy my party." He salutes and walks off.

Gemma grabs her stomach and whines, "I'm fucking hungry. Where's the food at?"

"Amira was supposed to be picking it up with Thanatos. I guess they're not back yet. I can grab you guys some beers while you wait, though," Calli offers. I snicker to myself as I think of it as an offering to appease the dragon. Gemma doesn't do well when she's hungry.

Calli walks over to the fridge and pulls it open, pulling out a beer for each of us. She slides them across the island to us all. "See, you had no need to really steal Hades' other than to be a bitch, Gemma."

"Who're you callin' a bitch, bitch?" Gemma says though she can't keep the smile off her face. I can never take her seriously with that shit.

She opens her beer, and I do the same.

"Cheers to Dad," Calli says, holding her beer up. Leave it to her to turn beer into something fancy.

"To Zeus," I say.

We all start to chug at the same time, getting us ready for the party ahead. The club can have some pretty raucous parties, and this will be no exception considering it's for the return of Zeus from the dead, really. Hopefully, I can avoid any more confrontations with Pan and just enjoy myself.

I follow Calli and Gemma back into the main area of the club. I look around and catch the vibe. Everyone's having a good time. Some are chatting, but some are already dancing with each other in the middle of the clubhouse, obviously having had a few beers already. Hades is still playing pool where Gemma left him, and he's clearly replaced the beer she took already. Hermes is over there with him, and Prez and Pan are nearby.

I really try not to overhear anything, considering how much trouble it got me into last time, but some of these guys have a loudmouth. Right now, that's saying something, considering it's already loud in here from the music and all the conversation, not to mention the pool balls hitting each other. So, why then is it that I can hear Pan mention the Vile Serpents? "Looks like Thorn's been hanging out at the old mill farm, based on what I've seen."

Poseidon chimes in, "Not exactly the place I would expect him to be, but I guess it's a way to lie low. I don't know, though. I think something's up."

Pan opens his mouth to say something else but then turns his neck to look around Poseidon and locks eyes with me. So much for avoiding conflict with him.

"Why the hell are you always eavesdropping? This is club business, and it has nothing to do with you. So, fuck off. "

My game face is on, and I shake my head. Why does he have to be so affronting? "Look, it's not my fault that you talk too loudly. Even with everything going on, I can hear you over everything else. Maybe you should work on that if you don't want someone to hear you."

Poseidon starts to laugh and covers his mouth, and I have to scrunch up my face not to react too. He's clearly getting a kick out of it. Though, Pan's clearly aggravated by it.

I roll my eyes and pull up my phone, deciding it's best to just scroll around in it for a bit. Maybe I can look up a good recipe I can try out for next Sunday's dessert. Give myself a challenge.

I try to drown out any more words that are being said by Pan so as not to piss him off further. I lean against the wall and scroll through several different recipes and blogs talking about unique desserts or twists on old-school recipes. Then, there's one that catches my eye.

"Gingersnap pumpkin pie," I mutter to myself. "Sounds pretty damn good, actually." I go through the recipe to see what the pie calls for and make sure it's not something bogus.

With a couple of healthier substitutions, I think it would be great and easy to make in bulk. I can throw several in the oven at once, and everyone loves a classic pumpkin pie, and this is a good twist on it. It's perfect.

I finish my beer and go to find where Gemma and Calli went. Calli's on the dance floor with Eros, and they look so damn cute. The two of them are completely inseparable. He's become a fixture at our house.

If Calli isn't at *Shots* or at the club with him, he's at home with us. I'm surprised that something hasn't been solidified yet, like a ring on her finger. Then again, I suppose they've been dealing with more pressing issues such as her father's health and Calli recovering from what happened to her.

An Usher song plays, and Gemma finds me quick, pulling me toward the dance floor with her. I look down at my shoes, knowing that I picked the wrong ones if I'm going to have to dance. I don't know how the hell Gemma does it in those stilettos. But these things I have on are bulky monsters. "Take those fucking things off," she yells at me, and I can tell she's already tipsy. She must've already had another beer or something else while I was scrolling on my phone.

I try not to think about what might've been done to this floor as I take my shoes off, leaving me barefoot other than a toe ring and an anklet. I let Gemma take me to the center of what's a makeshift dance floor. Really, it's nothing other than a space where everybody is bumping and grinding, but it works.

Gemma dances up on me, and I catch the vibe, grinding up on her. I know there are eyes on us, and it feels kind of good. I wonder if some of those eyes are Pan's or not. I wonder if he's thinking right now about what he's missed out on for being an ass.

After a couple of dances, Calli gets us more beer. I end up leaving my flannel somewhere in the club, I don't know where, as I get a little bit warmer from all the dancing and the alcohol. After a bit, I no longer give a shit about being barefoot either.

We almost forget about Pearl until she comes walking through the door, the only one of us right now who's sober. We all call to her from our spot at the bar right now, Cronos still trying to flirt with Gemma. Pearl comes over to us and looks at us, laughing. "It's almost like the whole party has happened without me. How am I gonna catch up?"

"Shots! Shots! Shots!" Gemma shouts out.

Pearl smiles, mostly because she can drink us all under the table even though she doesn't seem like the partying type. "All right, let's get some tequila, then," she announces.

Cronos, probably liking the idea of Gemma drunk, turns around and orders for us. He gets himself one too. The bartender passes them to us, and we all count to three before downing them and getting another round.

We're going to be getting tipsy super fast and staying that way for a while. That's for sure.

After more shots and more dancing, I'm feeling way too damn crowded and hot. I need some fresh air. I decide to go to the back, not wanting anyone to really follow me. I just need a few minutes of peace.

I exit into the lot where all the bikes are kept and look out across the small road that'll eventually lead out to the highway. Across from the lot to the left of the club is an expansive wooded area. A little path leads into it.

Call me a hippie, but I've always loved trees. I feel there's like this darkness and mystery to them that I can relate to. It definitely looks like somewhere I want to be right now. I head on to the little path and follow it inside.

The air smells like fresh wood and grass and the crunching leaves being turned into mulch underneath. The trees tower over me, some of them growing little mushrooms on them, some broken in places probably from storms and people and creatures.

I breathe in deep and then breathe out, grounding myself.

I take a few more steps into the woods when I'm grabbed from behind a tree. My mouth opens to scream, but a hand clasps over it, making it dry up in my throat. I can smell the whiskey on the guy. "I *so* don't fuckin' like you."

I relax, knowing the threat is only to my mental health. It's Pan. But he won't let go of my face.

I'm about to bite his finger when he finally lets me go. I turn around to face him and cross my arms over my chest, feeling much more vulnerable than I would expect as he looks at me. "You obviously must like me if you keep trying to prove yourself to me. And now you followed me out here."

Part of me wonders if it's like a kindergarten boy complex. I remember being told that the ones that push you down into the mud are the ones that really like you. It's a completely backward way of thinking, but maybe Pan's really that immature. In which case, I don't know if I can fault him for lying anymore. I guess he just doesn't know better.

"I don't give a fuck about what you think," Pan protests, and I just roll my eyes in response. It's clearly the opposite day or something.

"Pan, you keep trying to prove yourself to be a decent or good person or whatever type of man it is you want to look like, time and time again. And you scared the shit out of me to specifically pull me behind a tree to tell me that you don't like me. That screams of you giving a shit."

I think this guy just doesn't like to hear the truth about himself. But then again, a lot of men don't. Hell, a lot of people don't like to hear the truth, and I guess I can relate because hearing the truth after having been lied to for so long could be hard as hell.

"Trix, seriously, just shut up." I can't tell if it's more disgust or annoyance that's dripping off his tongue, but I'm ready to rip him a new asshole. I don't have to take this shit from him anymore, no matter my relation to anyone in the MC or what right he thinks he has to talk like this.

I bring out my fists, ready to strike, when he comes at me, his lips landing on mine. My body tenses, and it takes me a moment to relax and drop my hands. My lips automatically begin to move with his, our tongues lashing against each other inside our mouths.

His hand presses against my back, pushing me up against his body. The kiss is angry and intense, but it's also jaw-droppingly hot. In fact, I feel just about every emotion this asshole has ever felt as well as mine being released through this kiss, and damn if it isn't the most impactful kiss I've ever had in my life.

I don't want to forgive him. I don't want to let Pan back into my life, but I can't let go of whatever the hell this is between us either. Not now that I've fully felt it.

The kiss creeps up as a tingle, and electricity goes straight up and down through my whole body. I begin to warm up all over, my body turning into hot lava. Then the heat begins pooling together right in my center.

I fold to the kiss, and Pan backs me up against the tree. That's when I just let go. It feels like there's no choice, but then my heart and my body feel so free. I don't think I've felt that way in a long time.

His shirt is the first thing to come off. His lips detach from mine only for about a second or two as he rips his shirt off and throws it onto the ground, with no care about what happens to it. Then, it's his pants and my shirt. Simultaneously we chuck them off carelessly.

Each time we briefly reconnect and then remove another piece of clothing.

When my pants come down, he lifts me up, surprisingly strong for the fact that compared to some of the other guys, Pan's smaller. Don't get me wrong, he has some damn hot muscles, but he's shorter, leaner.

God, he's just sexy as hell, and I can't keep from giving in to him as much as I want to tell him to fuck off and be done with me.

My back is against the tree now, only my bra strap to protect me at all. There's no foreplay beyond that kiss, and luckily none needed, as he raises me over his waiting cock, pushing my panties out of the way.

If anyone were to walk out of the club and crane their necks over, they'd see us. I know they'll hear us because I keep sighing and moaning as he kisses up and down my collarbone.

"Fuck me," I tell him, and he looks into my eyes, holding my gaze. Why are anger and lust only a half-step away from each other?

He watches me closely as he plunges in, my mouth open in a scream as he digs deep, wasting no time impaling me with his cock.

He begins to bounce me up and down on him. His thrusts are desperate and hard. My insides scream, and so does my back as bark scrapes against it, making little cuts everywhere like a sex souvenir.

It kind of feels good, though. So many things have fucked me up in the head like this, and I'm so used to chaos and pain. Nobody knows it, not until they get me between the sheets.

Or between the branches, in this case.

"Fuck, yes!" I call out, wrapping my hands around his neck, my manicured nails threatening to break as I dig into his skin.

Pan grunts, punishing me for his own pain by biting down on the flesh at the left side of my neck.

I thrust my hips forward more, allowing him just that tiny bit deeper so he could slam all the way to the hilt. I see stars and lose all control of my senses.

His warmth against me is intoxicating, and it's so much better this way, totally raw.

I lean my head against the tree now, sweat dripping from every pore with our frantic motions. He hits that special spot over and over.

"Holy shit," he pants. "Fuck, you're so hot. You're so damn tight. You're wild," he tells me, and it becomes like a coaxing song that we both fuck each other to.

My legs begin to tremble around him, and he uses one arm to keep me there, growling like the damn wild god he is as he hits me over and over again inside, pressing for me to cum.

"Fuck, I'm gonna come. You've got to come now, baby. Come for me," he orders, and I just melt.

"I want you to fill me up," I tell him desperately. "I want you to let go inside me."

He slams in twice more before pressing me hard into the tree, lashing us together as he roars. His warmth spills inside me, and damn, that's all I need to reach fulfillment, electricity and throbbing wracking my center.

Tears fill my eyes with the level of pleasure almost too much to handle.

My pulsing milks him dry again, and my eyes roll back in my head, allowing the feel of him to just sit there still inside of me for a moment.

"We need to go back to my room," he announces gruffly.

"Why?" I pant as he finally lets me go, my legs like jelly as my feet land back on the ground. My world sways as I try to catch my bearings.

Pan turns around and starts gathering our clothes in a bundle. He throws mine into my arms, and I barely catch them, still half numb and tingling from what we just did.

"Cause you're gonna scream louder in round two, and I want to give you the decency of privacy."

Chills run up and down my spine at the idea of doing that all over again.

I nod and tug my clothes back on, my body already begging for more just looking at him.

The hunger I feel for him is insatiable, and I hardly notice anyone as we come through the back and head straight for the stairs up into the living quarters. For one second, I think about trying to grab my shoes and flannel, but then I figure I'll deal with it later. This is more important right now.

The whole time, my eyes are on Pan's back, watching as his muscles move up and down with his steps.

I think about all the positions he could take me in, and my breath catches in my chest. He turns to look at me once, the look in his eyes predatory and shining with more lust than I can handle.

My breath comes in shallow bursts as we come to the door to his room. He pushes it open, and I practically leap inside of it, the door shutting behind us with a soft thud.

I don't try to notice any details. That's not important right now. As much as I'd like to psychoanalyze his space and find out why he is the way he is, I'd rather him fuck me senseless.

He walks up to me, pinning my arms over my head against the door, his body pressed against mine. One of his hands gently trails down my body with the touch of a feather, waking up every nerve until I feel I might explode.

I whimper, and he grins. "Get undressed and get on the bed," he growls.

I like a man who takes charge, not necessarily a Dom, but one who is clear about what he wants and how he wants it and can give me enough. So, I let the fact he's ordering me around go and obey.

I want what he does anyway.

I sit naked on the edge of the bed now, no panties or bra even in the way this time. I spread my legs wide, so he could see my pretty, pink center waiting for him, dripping wet and probably soaking his bed in my scent.

He'll have to smell me when he goes to sleep tonight.

He comes close, standing between my legs. His shirt is already off, but he undoes his jeans and slides them down with his boxers to his ankles. His cock is still hard, and from this angle, I can see he's thick.

I wonder for a moment as my mouth waters if I could fit him all in or not.

Just for fun, I lash my tongue across his shaft, sliding upward and back down again. He shivers at my touch.

I do the same to the other side, and then he stops me.

"Fuck, as good as that feels, and as much as I want you to finish the job sometime, I'd like to be inside you again."

The way his voice is so low and husky almost makes me orgasm right there. The want he has for me; I don't know why I haven't seen it underneath all of his attitude. It's plain as day now.

I spread my legs a little wider, inviting him in.

He surprises me by reaching down and grabbing each of my legs to hike them up, forcing me to lay down on the bed, my ass sliding to the very edge.

He looks down at me with a sly grin as he places each of my legs around his waist, and I use the leverage to pull him tight against me. His cock enters me slightly because of my movement, maybe a few inches.

He chuckles darkly at me and then grabs my hips, using them to thrust himself the rest of the way in.

I call out, and I'm so damn loud I doubt being upstairs from the party is even going to drown out what the hell we're doing. By morning, everyone could know I fucked Pan.

Unable to do anything else, I fist his bedsheets, trying not to entirely rip them off his bed as he pulls me a little further off the edge, my hips angled high for a deeper penetration.

He just sits in there, letting me get used to the feeling of him and waiting for me to beg for mercy.

I stare at him, waiting for him to give in first. And he does.

He pulls out almost all the way only to slam in again, and again, and again.

"Pan. Fuck."

"It's so good to fuck your tight pussy. I love how you like to feel all of me inside you," he tells me. "How I get to feel all of you."

He fucks me hard and fast, and I squint my eyes shut, all the colors of the rainbow flashing behind them with the overload of ecstasy. I'm in for a lot of trouble, but this is my new addiction.

CHAPTER FOUR

PAN

I wake up not knowing exactly what time it is but knowing instantly that something's different. A flood of memories comes back to me from yesterday, and I have to sort through each one of them to get a grip on how I feel.

No one knows it about me, but my emotions can be unstable. They get gloomy and dark, like a storm cloud rolls in and follows me around and won't go away.

Things between Trix and me are intense. I just haven't been able to figure out whether that intensity is positive or negative. But if last night didn't solidify it for me, I don't know what will.

Shit, I feel myself getting turned on just thinking about it all over again.

I'm lying on my back, and I stretch carefully, so I don't wake her up. Having her in here is surreal.

Something should look different. It's like there's been a shift in the universe. But the same acoustic guitar leans against the wall farthest from me. Everything, even the dark curtains, is still in their places other than the rumpled white sheets we're laying on.

Then, I slowly turn over and see that she's on her side, facing away from me. I see the little cuts from where I fucked her against the tree yesterday, and I'm tempted to kiss each and every one.

The center of her back is covered with a large tattoo. It's gorgeous, and I immediately notice it's Medusa.

She's beautiful, sultry. Her lips are puckered sensually, and her arms invite you in. But of course, snakes swirl around her head, letting you know that she's not just some woman to use and abuse. She'll kill you as easily as bring you pleasure.

I don't know if Trix is just into Greek mythology or if there's more to it. If nothing else, it lets me know that Trix is definitely a strong woman and one not to be messed with. It's exactly what's both infuriating and attractive about her. She takes control in a way other women just don't. At least not the women that I've been around before. It's going to make whatever this thing we have going on a hell of a lot more complicated than what I'm used to. But I think she's worth the trouble.

I can't help but begin to trace the shapes of the snakes. The fluidity of the art shows all of the shadows on Medusa's face. The artist did a brilliant job, and it doesn't need any color for it to really stand out.

Trixie wakes up gently to me doing this. I see the corner of her smile spreading across her face. "This is beautiful," I tell her, though I don't just mean the tattoo.

We lay there in silence for a little bit longer, soaking in the good feelings of the night before and the calm before Trix breaks it. Because, of course, she has to. "Why do you think we've started arguing so much lately?" she asks me.

I straight up start cackling. Of all the things to ask me first thing in the morning after we just fucked like rabbits twice . . . she wants to talk about us arguing. An argument that apparently meant very little considering the way our bodies meshed together the night before.

"It's you who had the attitude with me first," I tease her, tickling the tattoo a little now. She squirms under my touch and turns over, revealing her bare body to me. I try not to stare too hard because I know we won't get to finish this conversation, and instead, I'll be taking her all over again.

And I doubt that's really a fucking option, even though Zeus would totally understand where I was coming from because, with Zeus back, he's going to want to talk about what's been going on while Hades has been in control. No one stressed him out with the details of what happened. He knows Calli was taken, but nothing else.

I'm sure he forced Hades to fill him in first thing this morning, not even letting him sleep in because of a hangover, which I'm sure Hades had. Considering how much he had to drink the night before, it wouldn't be shocking in the least bit. I'm surprised Trix doesn't have one because I saw her knocking them back too.

"I did," Trix admits, "but it's because you were totally on board for lying to Calli about how bad Zeus was. It was really lucky that he turned out to be okay, but he could've died. And you helped lie about it to her. That could have turned out totally different. I just couldn't let my friend not know the truth. It's not right."

From her standpoint, she's not wrong. Her knowing about it and not saying something is a different situation entirely than me knowing about it and not saying anything. I was following a direct order, not to mention that while Calli is an amazing woman, and I love her as one of my best friend's ol' ladies, I don't have the same connection to her that Trix does. I'm not her best friend, her roommate. I don't know the same things that Trix, Eros, and Gemma all would.

I probably could've saved us some fights from seeing that early on. Both our sides had good reasons, but as I said before, my emotions aren't that stable or easy to see beyond. Not to mention, I have to admit that it was all of that built-up anger and frustration that was able to make last night like fireworks.

I sigh. "You won't agree with the club shit all the time. But the thing is, if you're going to be around here like this more often if you're going to be around me, you'll have to learn to respect it. I literally don't have a choice in the matter. This is my family, just like Calli and Gemma are yours."

Trix settles herself on her back, places her hands on her stomach and stares up at the ceiling. My eyes roam her body, and I bite my lip. I stay quiet, letting her think, but it goes on for so long that I'm a little afraid she's just going to walk away, but then she says, "I do respect it. But again, you can't expect me to like it, especially if it involves lying. And I'm not a member, so I don't necessarily have to comply."

I leave it alone because, if she's shown me anything, it's that she isn't the type of woman who will blindly follow in order. She's going to ask questions. And she's still probably going to question me even if she can respect that I have to act a certain way or follow a certain rule. But I kind of like the challenge of her. It's making my life a little bit less boring.

I scoot myself a little closer to her and decide to change the subject. "So, I saw that tattoo on your back. It's totally wicked, some of the best black and white art I've seen, but is there a meaning to it? I mean, are you just into mythology, or is there something behind it?"

Trix sits up in bed so that I get it in full view again, though I can't help but follow my eyes down to the curve of her ass as she leans over to find her clothes and put them on. "It's really not important. I don't know that you'd get it."

I sit up and straddle her from behind, kissing her back and neck. Goosebumps break out all over her skin, even as she tries to ignore me while attempting to get dressed. I'm just greatly amused by the fact that I'm making it that much harder for her. I could look at her all day. "Come on, try me. It makes me curious about you."

She stands up and pulls her pants the rest of the way on, starting to button them when she says, so nonchalantly that I don't take it seriously at first, "It's because I was raped as a child."

If it's a joke, it's a fucking sick thing to joke about, but I've heard worse. This is an MC, after all. But as I give her time to clear the air or refute it, and she doesn't even meet my gaze, I know she's telling the truth.

Shit, she isn't kidding at all.

"I need to get going. No offense, I just have a cake to get decorated today for our client." I'm stunned to silence as I watch her finish putting on her clothes and then just walk out without another word being said to me. The door shuts behind her, and the weight of the shit that she admitted to me starts to sit on my chest like a ton of bricks.

Trix doesn't look or act like the kind of girl that I thought had that kind of dark thing in her past. Not that from the surface, I look like a guy who gets depressed and can't get rid of the dark cloud over him. I guess we do all have our demons, but I just never expected her to say that. Otherwise, I never would've pushed her to tell me what the tattoo was all about.

I assumed she felt whatever the meaning behind it was silly, not that it was something serious like this.

I hope I haven't fucked up with her over this by not reacting in the right way. I'll have to make sure that we talk about it sometime, but for now, I know I need to get out of bed and head downstairs. As much as Zeus likes to party, he'll want to get back to work right away.

I put my clothes back on and note that the scent of my clothes and my room all smell like Trix and me together. It's intoxicating, but I'll probably still have to wash everything up when I get back up here.

As soon as I get downstairs, I don't even get to go grab some oatmeal or some shit for breakfast before Zeus calls church. Hades is right next to him, and I realize I must have been right. Zeus got filled in either last night or first thing this morning.

He's going to immediately want to go after the Vile Serpents. It's just a matter of figuring out where they are and what they're up to.

I file into church with the other boys, trying to clear my mind of the scent and feeling of Trix up against me. There's a lot of bullshit about Zeus being back and how we're going to get our revenge. Normally stuff I'd be enthusiastic about hearing, but I just can't seem to get the shit with Trix off my mind. It's like trying to wade through molasses.

"Thorn and his boys have definitely been doing some shit at the Millers' farm." It's those words from Zeus that snap me out of it. So, I guess my intel was right. I had uncovered at least Thorn, if not some of the Vile Serpents. What the hell they were doing there beats me, though.

Zeus continues, "I don't want to move too slow on this. I want to go in hard and hot when they don't expect us. I don't want them to be able to change their plans. Thorn needs to pay. They all fuckin' do."

Hades steps up, giving his two cents. "We all ride in an hour. Well, all of us but Zeus. Since you almost died once and we don't want to lose you, I think you should stay back. You're our Prez, so you can do whatever the hell you want, but as more than just your VP but also as your friend, I'd rather you not risk it. Your daughter probably feels the same."

Zeus looks like he's about ready to cut his head off, surprise surprise. He isn't usually one for resting. It's a miracle he stayed in the hospital even while he was dying and didn't force himself to be signed out. "Respectfully, Hades, go fuck yourself. Everybody get ready to roll out."

CHAPTER FIVE

TRIX

Shit. What in the hell is wrong with me?

No matter what I do, I haven't been able to shake Pan off my mind. I want to get him out of my head. It's not good for me to obsess over a guy like this, especially one that now knows my darkest secret—inadvertently, of course.

He pressed too hard to know about that damn tattoo, and then I didn't know what to say when I admitted everything. I mean, how do you explain that kind of trauma to someone who has seen so much death and just laughs it off? The simple answer: you don't. Then again, I shouldn't have to explain myself to him. I don't owe him any explanations.

But every time I close my eyes, all I can see is the way he looks at me with hunger-filled eyes. I can remember every way he touched me and exactly what it felt like. But I can't seem to replicate it my damn self. It just sucks.

I guess this means I'm going to have to see him again, which means I risk Gemma finding out. Well, not risk. It's not something I'll hide from her forever. I'm not going to turn myself into a liar. I wouldn't be able to look at myself in the mirror. But with any new relationship, I have to figure things out before I go blabbing my mouth. I don't even know what he wants other than my body.

"I'll meet you in the car!" Calli calls from down the hall, shutting her bedroom door. We're supposed to be having a girl's day at *Shots*. She actually has the night off, and so do I, now that I'm done with that last order, so we're going to do happy hour. Gemma's going to join us when she gets off work too. I feel like we're always busy with guys and work these days. We don't spend enough time with each other. And she's even convinced Pearl to go, and Pearl never goes anywhere.

Pearl's an amazing roommate for many reasons, but she's really the quiet type. She prefers books and movies versus clubs and alcohol, though she can definitely hold her own when she does let loose. But we deserve a girls' day, and here I'm thinking about someone that I probably shouldn't be. And I'm so not ready to make it a top of conversation with all of us.

I adjust my crop top and let my hair down, finger-combing through it a bit. Then, I go ahead and head out to the car, Pearl comes out of her room and heads out right behind me.

We both climb into Callis' car, and then we're off. Calli puts on some great mood music getting us ready. We're blasting Britney Spears with the windows down and singing along when we pull up to *Shots*. Feeling a little more myself, I follow them inside, and we get our seats.

We immediately order a small appetizer, shots, and a beer each. It's a good start, and happy hour is cheap enough for us to keep them coming.

Pearl sips her drink slowly, already having told us she's not that into drinking today. It's fine with Calli and me since she can be the designated driver at the end of this.

Calli and I have already made a deal that we're getting completely hammered. YOLO and all that shit, right?

Calli and I are already tipsy by the time Gemma shows up. Gemma is ready to go, already complaining about her work day when she comes and sits with us. We each do a jager bomb, clinking them together to celebrate another day of work finished and the weekend coming.

It's incredibly fun, and I steer clear of the topic of Pan. Everyone else makes it easy since they don't really bring him up. In fact, we don't bring up guys at all.

Around 7:00, we end up ordering some more food to sober up with. Never want to be knee-walking drunk walking out of here. Even if we're in a group, a bunch of women driving alone drunk is not a good idea. Besides, Gemma does have to drive her truck alone.

After the food arrives at our table, I look around the bar just to see who's here, and out of the corner of my eye, I spot a cut I haven't seen before. I do a double-take as I realize it says Iowa on one of the patches.

A shiver runs down my spine, and I try not to show that I'm shaken, but I am.

If someone asks, I'll be the first to admit that I have a lot of trauma that I haven't necessarily dealt with in the healthiest ways. And having a reminder of the place where I was dumped at a fire station at a couple of days old, thus launching me into the life that I led up until I finally left all of it and could make something of myself, it's not exactly something I'm happy about. But there it is, in plain sight, glaring at me as if teasing me.

As far as I'm concerned, Iowa is a hellhole I'll never go back to.

Though seeing someone from there gets me a little bit curious, in a dangerous way, and I should know better. But I look anyway. I turn and try to get a good look at the man's face, just in case. But the minute I see his dark green eyes and white beard, I know.

I know it's him, and I know my past has officially come back to haunt me.

I feel instantly sick, and I don't know if I can stay here another second. Nausea and pain fill my whole body at the thought.

"Shit, I left my phone charger back at the club. Trix, Pearl, either of you wanna come to the club with me to go grab it?"

The walls are closing in around me. In a croaking voice I say, "Yes, I'll go." I get up and walk out, trying not to make a scene by doing it too quickly. As much as I want out of here right now, I don't want to catch his eye the way he's caught mine. I just want to go and get out of here safely.

I want him to go back to the hellhole he crawled out of and then pretend like I never had to encounter him again, even from afar.

CHAPTER SIX

PAN

We all make it off the bikes, cuts on us to show who we are. If we have to raid the farm and go after these assholes, we want the last thing they see to be us, Sons of Gods MC, fucking them over for what they did to our Prez and our Princess.

By some miracle, Hades has gotten Zeus to agree to stay behind and been given the proverbial reins to handle all of us for this.

Zeus is on light duty after all, and maybe as much as it pissed him off, that final comment about Calli being upset if he got hurt again hit him where it hurt. I know it would me.

We all climb on our bikes, revving the engines and slowly taking formation. I'm right behind the officers other than Cronos, our road captain who takes the lead, and Hades, who holds up the rear so he can give orders as needed.

We take to the road and head out of Birmingham toward the farm.

The Millers own a 20-acre farm about 10 miles out of Birmingham. Their main deal is beef cattle and the few crops needed to feed the cattle and the family. The Millers have always been known as homebodies. Most people never see them unless it's necessary for them to grab something in town.

Even for farmers, they've always been kind of weird.

Hades let it slip as we were getting ready that Thorn knows one of the Miller boys, so that connection must be allowing him to lay low there for a bit.

It's a large fuckin place, so there's no telling if it's only Thorn himself who's hiding there or if he could have his officers or even more of the club there with him.

"You think they're there preparing for a fight?" I ask Hermes over the roar of the road. I still can't believe all my snooping has led to a solid lead. I haven't been a fully patched member that long, and I'm making my club proud.

Somehow, my thoughts go to Trix, and I want to tell her how this makes me feel. She might get more comfortable with the MC shit if I share more of it with her.

I can't get too distracted right now, though.

"I would fuckin' bet my life on it. Those bastards wouldn't completely tuck tail, not with crazy-ass Thorn leading them. What they don't know is he's leading them straight into hell."

I smile at the thought. These fuckers will get what's been coming to them all along.

The ride felt short, and we saw the windmill, an old-fashioned kind of forest, and then a few bikes parked on the sandy gravel. This is the right damn place. How could they be so careless?

So much for fucking hiding out!

We make to pass the farm, and then Cronos gives the signal along with Hades from the back. We slow down and head toward a pull-off next to a patch of woods a lot like the ones that keep our own clubhouse more secluded.

We kill the engines, making it seem like we were just driving past. No one inside should think anything else about the noise if we play our cards right.

We all walk our bikes into the woods, hidden from the street. No one even pulling out will be able to see we're here and that there's so fucking many of us. We're going to come up on them like a sudden storm in the middle of the night.

Adrenaline pulses through my veins as I join Hades and a few others, awaiting further orders.

We gather our teams, Poseidon and Kratos leading the others as Hades gives his official orders.

"You're going to take your team and head around the back. Go around the barn. I don't want anyone trying to fuckin' escape and actually getting away if we can help it. We need to nip this in the bud."

A collective grunt comes from all of us. We all want to be done with these fuckers for good. They deserve to be punished, and I don't want any more trouble from them to come to us, especially after what Calli has been through.

"We'll rush them from the cornfield," he tells our group and me. "It's not ideal other than the fact it'll give us cover going in. The element of surprise is crucial here. Let's get 'em, boys."

There's murder in his eyes, and I know Hades is going to be responsible for a lot of enemies down today. I plan to make it a point to be right there with him.

Poseidon confirms his boys know what they need to do and heads off, leaving us to go up to the treeline with Hades in the lead.

We move swiftly, quietly, in short bursts so as not to be detected through the brush. We squat down to check and make sure nothing is happening, and no one has been alerted of our presence before continuing every few yards.

We get so close we can hear talking, and all of us spread out a little, guns at the ready as we crouch down in the brush.

Hades and I are closest to where the members of the Vile Serpents sit, lounging as if they haven't done anything wrong. How they sleep, I have no fuckin' idea.

"You know, the next time Thorn sees Zeus, he's gonna finish him off. Can't believe that cockroach motherfucker survived it."

Hades looks over at me. He's heard it too. His face is practically turning purple with rage. What the hell? They're seriously shitting on our Prez that they nearly killed. Not paying the price for any fuckin' thing and not worried that we could come for them. Maybe they don't know Zeus is out of the hospital, or maybe they just don't give a shit.

It's disrespectful as fuck. I don't know how they can wear cuts and patches and behave the way they do. MCs have a way in which they behave. It's about camaraderie. Protection. Even when it comes to enemies, that's just supposed to be territorial shit. Not busting into a birthday party at a neutral bar to kill the Prez over a woman that was being assaulted and didn't take it anymore.

Hades gives the signal, and my adrenaline pumps blood up to my ears as we all stand, guns blazing.

Hades goes straight for the asshole who popped his fuckin' mouth off and gets him between the eyes.

Many of the Serpents are unprepared, not thinking they'd be found here, I guess. As they scramble for their guns and try to shout orders and for help, we shoot each one of them in the chest, head, stomach, wherever we know will kill them.

Bullets begin to fly back and forth both ways, and I force myself not to turn and run because I know we have justice on our side and are winning.

Serpents members, including the backup rushing in from somewhere inside the place, begin to fall to the ground in pools of their own blood. I don't stop to see if we have any injuries. I have to focus on this right now.

Some nasty-looking motherfucker with a snake tongue sticking out at me, and every inch of him covered in tats aims straight at me. I feel the wind clip me as the bullet flies past, barely missing me. I step toward him and pop two shots off, watching his surprise as he falls.

It's like these assholes thought they were all getting away with what they did to ours, what they did to a woman, for that matter. They thought they were so damn clever hiding out at a farm and chilling like it would all blow the hell over.

A couple of the injured grab their guns from where they dropped them and aim at Hades. I don't hesitate to shoot one in the chest while Hades gets the other one on the right side of his forehead. Like this, they're all on an even playing field, meeting their maker.

Finally, only one stands. I can't say there aren't more members somewhere, especially Thorn, but a large chunk of them are now dead, the Vile Serpents crippled now.

It's at least a start.

Hades points his gun at the remaining member, a pudgy man who is likely just a member if not a prospect.

He's practically shivering with fear.

"You're going to talk. You're going to tell us where to find Thorn and what the hell he's up to, or you're going to go to hell with the rest of your buddies." Hades grits his teeth and walks up to the body of one of the deceased members, kicking it in disrespect. There's blood now smeared on the front of his boot.

"I can't. I'd rather die than tell you shit. The punishment would be worse than death." Before I can lunge and grab him, he puts his gun to his head and blows his fuckin' brains all over the place.

I have a pretty damn strong stomach, but the space spins for a moment, and I feel like I might hurl. That's fuckin' sick, and it was only a foot away from me.

"Fuck!" Hades yells, kicking at dead bodies and splashing guts and blood and bullets everywhere. "We're back to fuckin' square one!" He was right.

"Whatever Thorn does to punish these guys must be pretty damn bad," I comment, swallowing bile.

The other guys come back to us as we head back toward our bikes. I begin to do a mental headcount and see that while a couple of the guys have minor wounds and a lot of dirt and blood on them, we're all alive and relatively fine. No one even looks like they can't just drive outta here.

Hades kicks rocks and curses as he turns around, having his personal tantrum, and I can't blame him. I wouldn't want to be the one to go back and tell Zeus that while they're all dead, he knows nothing more than we did before.

Hermes walks over to me and points, a grim look on his face. "You okay?"

"What?" I look down where he's pointing and see my right arm where a bullet has grazed. There's a nasty laceration there, it probably needs stitches, and it's bleeding.

"Shit, I didn't even feel it," I admit. "Fuck." It must have been that one fucker with all the tats. It didn't miss me as much as I thought it had. I almost had a date with the devil, it looks like. But I won for today.

I wonder what Trix is gonna think, though. I know she has some qualms about things already. Well, shit.

Hades points toward where we've parked our bikes. "Let's get you back to the club and get it patched up."

"Yeah, I don't think there's any other choice. Don't see any first aid around here," I say, following everyone back to the bikes.

I climb on, the adrenaline fading as I realize it does sting some, especially where the wind hits it. It's going to be a shitty ride back to the club, that's for sure.

We ride out, no longer afraid of anyone hearing us, a partial victory hanging over our heads in a strange mix of feelings.

It feels like it takes forever as my arm bleeds even more on the way home.

Once we park, Kratos comes up to me. "Get inside. I'll take care of it."

I go straight to the bar to wait for him while he gets the kit. I might need some drinks to handle what comes next.

I look down at it and see that it looks worse now that it's been sitting there for like half an hour.

The sound of footsteps on the stairs gets my attention, thinking it might be Zeus, but instead, it's Calli and Trix. Fuck, it's the last thing she'll want to see or know about.

Our eyes meet, and I'm just waiting for the reaction.

CHAPTER SEVEN

TRIX

"Got it," Calli says, pulling her charger out of the plug in the wall next to her bed. Or rather, the wall next to Eros' bed. It's practically her bed, though. She spent about half the week with us and the other half with him. They're practically inseparable, which is pretty darn cute if you ask me.

"So now what?" I ask her, still reeling from the events of earlier. My past slapped me hard in the face, and I'm kind of in the mood to make sure that I get my mind off of it and stay away from it. I'm trying to keep my mind from going into the mode of needing to chop my hair off and die it a crazy color so I'm unrecognizable. But hopefully, it's a one-time problem. Hopefully, he was just visiting, and he'll disappear for years on end again.

"You know, some hibachi sounds good. I know I saw a good place along the highway I've been meaning to try. Have you ever been there?" Calli asks as we make our way to the stairs to go back down into the main part of the clubhouse.

Before I can answer, we hear some noise. We had been alone for the most part, other than a few people like Zeus in the clubhouse. I don't exactly have the privilege of knowing what they're doing regardless of who I'm sleeping with, but I assume that they're all out doing some kind of reconnaissance mission in regard to the assholes that shot Zeus up at Calli's birthday party. But they must be back because there's a lot of commotion coming from downstairs.

"Yeah, I've been there a couple of times with Gemma before you moved in with us. It's pretty damn good. But we better see what all the shit is downstairs first."

Calli groans and I can see how her stomach's twisted in knots over whatever it is that's going on. She doesn't show it a lot on the outside, but I know she must worry about Eros. He's clearly the love of her life, and every time he leaves to deal with the Serpents, they might find the Serpents and then find themselves being shot in just the same way Zeus was.

And she had almost lost her father already, the one she just got back. I don't know if she would be able to survive losing Eros on top of that.

I'm incredibly proud to have this strong friend, but strength only goes so far. My life tells me that, but I don't ever plan on being weak again.

We go down the stairs to see that there's quite a bit of chaos. There are a few members dirty, clothes tattered, or covered in blood. Nobody seems to be that seriously injured except for one person.

I lock eyes with Pan at the bar, and I can see the injury from a mile away. He has a huge, red laceration on his arm, and it's bleeding. There are splashes of dry blood everywhere on his upper arm, and as I get closer, I realize that his skin looks to be completely shredded.

What the hell happened?

"Calli, come on, what the fuck?" I ask in shock as I point over to Pan. Here's this guy I've been sleeping with, and he's got some kind of huge ass injury, and everyone is just acting like it's normal. Shouldn't he be in the hospital?

I shake my head, feeling like an idiot.

Of course, he can't go to the hospital. They'll ask where he got it and have to explain he's in a motorcycle club, which I doubt will go over well.

Calli and I walk up to him and looking at the wound, I can tell it was probably a bullet that grazed him. Thank God it didn't pierce through. It could have gone into any major artery in the upper arm. It's not really a good place for a bullet.

Of course, is there such a thing as a good place for a bullet? This life is crazy as fuck.

"Pan, what the hell happened? I can tell this is from a bullet," I gesture to the injury.

"Kratos went to go get the first aid kit." He looks up at me and smirks as if he's getting some kind of entertainment from me giving a shit. Honestly, though, he probably is.

It's not like I know every inch of him at this point, while not mentally anyway, but I know enough about him to know he would probably be getting a kick out of this. I guess the pain can't be that bad then, can it?

"Don't make me ask you again. What the hell happened to you? It's not a fucking joke."

He takes a swig of something, probably whiskey from the smell of it. I realize they must be doing some kind of a patch job on it, and he's preparing himself, but alcohol when you're bleeding just makes me cringe. It's a bad idea.

But I guess it can't be the first injury they've dealt with this way.

"Good to know you give a damn, but I got grazed by a bullet. It was nothing serious."

Calli puts her hands on her hips. "Even I know better than that. If this is all over getting revenge on Thorn, it needs to stop. I don't want people getting killed on my watch because of something that was done to me. And he tried to kill my father too, I get it, but it's not worth us dying over. I'm going to go get my dad and ask what he wants us to do. And maybe have a little conversation with him."

"Good luck with that. We have a vendetta to pay back to them, Calli. They've wronged us, and it shows weakness if it goes unpunished. Every damn MC in Alabama will be after us if we back down," Pan explains to her.

She fixes him with a stare, and then Calli walks off, leaving him temporarily alone. I look sympathetically after her, knowing she isn't going to hear anything she likes from Zeus, her father or not. He's the Prez. It's clear to me that all of them will stick to the rules no matter the risks because it's a calculated gamble not to make the risks higher for them.

They protect each other. I think it's what Pan has been trying to tell me. I still don't personally get it, but there's no messing with it either.

Everybody seems to be scrambling to get new clothes on and get rid of any evidence, I suppose. I try not to think about what the other side must look like. Considering I'm not in front of the only person that seems to be seriously intruding at all, the blood must be from all of them.

"I can't believe you're drinking and just acting like this shit isn't a big deal. Your skin is shredded, Pan. Do you not get that? And if you got grazed by a bullet, it means it could have been much worse than this. Don't you give a shit about anything?" I ask him, furious. Who acts like this isn't a big deal anyway? It's a damn big deal.

And I get they're all supposed to be these tough guys, but tough in the face of severe injury by a bullet, tough in the face of death? I don't fucking know about that.

Kratos finally shows up with his first aid kit. It's a substantial wound, but in his hand, all he holds is a spool of black thread and a needle, like actual black thread for patching up clothing and stuffed animals.

I press my fingers into my temples and try not to scream, but their idiocy is giving me a headache. I glare at Kratos, and he seems to notice and kind of steps back and looks me over. "What is it?" he asks, looking himself up and down as if maybe there's something crawling on him.

The only thing I see crawling on him, though, is the bug of stupidity.

"And what exactly do you plan on doing with that?" I ask him, waiting for his medical explanation. I'm going to love hearing this.

Kratos just raises his brows at me in response. "Damn, I like your spiciness." Oh Lord, he's flirting with me. He's flirting with me when Pan is bleeding and has a huge hole in his arm.

"She's spoken for," Pan butts in, and my eyes bug out for a second. Not only are Kratos and Pan staring each other down right now, and I'm pretty sure Kratos has more of a say in the MC than Pan does, but Pan basically just claimed me.

I don't know what to think of that, considering that he's still got a gaping wound from a graze from a bullet, and I have no idea how he got it. I don't have the details of what happened.

There's a tightness in my core, and if I'm being honest, as much as I hate the idea of being owned by someone, the way he just shut Kratos up like that is kind of hot. I mean, it also kind of lets me know where I stand without having to ask, which is nice.

But right now, I need to focus. There's no way in hell I'm going to let Kratos go sewing up open, shredded skin like that with a regular needle and thread as if he's sewing a button on a vest.

I ignore the two of them and look at Kratos. I don't even meet eyes with Pan once during the awkwardness. I store it away in the back of my brain for another time. "If you do it that way, you will give him a raging infection. You're going to go find a fishing line and bring it back to me. There's got to be at least one biker in this club who has some inner hick in him. So find it so I can fix what you were about to entirely screw up."

I can tell Kratos is offended, but he covers it up with a little whistle as he walks away. Pan begins to chuckle. "I don't know how the hell you're laughing through this, maybe it's the alcohol, which by the way, is not a good idea, but seriously, Pan, are you okay?"

I look him up and down with worry. It's kind of a wake-up call that I'm so scared about whether or not he's okay right now. I mean, of course, seeing anyone injured is awful, but there's something different about this feeling. I may be in deeper with him than I ever suspected.

"Seriously, I'm fine. The wind stung on the way here, but you can see the bleeding slowed down a lot. I'm drinking because of the pain. We're going to get me patched up. But now that I think about it, how do you know to use a fishing line to suture me up? "

I almost shut down. I can feel my eyes going kind of dark, my expression emotionless as I school it to be that way, so I don't lose my shit. I push back all those dark memories from my past and hope that Pan doesn't notice that little blip.

I guess he hasn't noticed the scars on my legs yet. I mean, we did only fuck in the dark. If we ever do it in the light, he'll definitely see it eventually. "That's a conversation for another day. Let's worry about you right now."

Kratos comes back with a fishing line, looking a little bit amused now. "So, I guess you are the hick one, huh?" I tease, taking it from him. I pull the first aid kit that he set down on the bar next to me and start going through it. I pull out the betadine. "I'll also need a bottle of tequila, please."

Kratos hops behind the bar to grab one, passing it to me. It's mostly full, though I can tell a couple of shots have been had from it. I open it and take a swig for myself, and then I hand it to Pan. "I know you've been drinking whiskey, but I don't think it's gonna cut it. Take a few shots of this to ease the pain. This is going to be a while."

Pan shakes his head, takes the bottle from me, and slams it back down on the counter. "I can handle it. Let's just get this over with. You said it yourself that it's not good to keep drinking right now."

So now he cares to listen to me?

I fix him with a stare. I doubt he's going to feel that way in a few minutes, but there's really no choice. I glance inside the first aid kit and grab the curved needle. Thank goodness there's one of these in here. Otherwise, this would be a whole heck of a lot worse.

I douse the needle in betadine and then thread it with the fishing line.

"Okay, what I'm going to need to do is make sutures that are not connected. I'm going to start in the middle and go out. You're going to have to be very still, do you understand?" I ask him.

"Yes, ma'am." I glare at him for a moment, not appreciating the joke, and then I use my left hand to pinch his skin together. I take the needle and push through a piece of flesh on the left, pull through, and then go through on the right. I begin to tie it off, and then I tie it off again, making sure that the tied part is to one side of the injury and not right in the middle.

As I go through the motions, placing them only about a centimeter apart, he makes a couple of noises under his breath but nothing more. He's also perfectly still.

Pan is clearly much braver than I was when I had to do this to myself years ago. Then again, he's not having to do it himself, and he probably feels pretty damn safe here.

I'm surprised that my hands don't shake thinking about it, and so we get done in about 10 or 15 minutes. I pick up the betadine once more and douse the whole thing in it. Then, I rub some antibiotic ointment and then rub another layer on to be certain. I hate that we're having to do it here and not at a hospital. But at least this way, if there is an infection in part of it, that suture can be removed without removing all of them.

I go into the first aid kit again and grab the gauze. I wrap his arm with the gauze and then an ace bandage to protect it. "You know, you're kind of hot when you get all doctor-like," Pan says, though I have to lean in close to hear him.

I try not to smile at it because I don't want to encourage him to behave this way when he's got an injury. What if it's worse next time? "I'm definitely not a doctor."

"Could have fooled me," he says

I pull away and look down. "You should really get some rest."

I get the feeling his stubborn ass is not going to do it, though. Instead, he smiles at me and asks, "Why don't you come upstairs with me."

I should say no, but I know I'm going to give in. Even if it's just because I'm worried and I kind of want to get the whole story if he'll give it to me. "Go ahead, and I'll be up in a few. I have to find where Calli is and tell her I won't be going out with her for hibachi."

He nods and then follows my directions to go upstairs at least. I start looking through the club downstairs, and I find Calli talking with her father. "Hey, how is he?" Calli asks.

"He's stitched up and covered up. It's the best I can do right now. Good fucking thing I was here, though, considering Kratos was about to cause a massive infection by using regular cloth thread and a regular needle."

"You're staying with him, aren't you?" Calli asks, and I just nod. She's making it easy on me, at least. She's kind of good at the no judgment thing.

"Should I say something to Gemma?" Calli asks. I hadn't even thought of that.

"Don't tell her right now. I'm not going to hide it from her. I'll tell her something soon. It's just really fresh, and you know she's gonna freak the fuck out. Plus, I want to get the whole story out of him first."

Calli smiles. "Okay, have fun."

I roll my eyes at her and flip her off. "Fuck off, Calli." But I'm smiling the whole damn time.

CHAPTER EIGHT

PAN

I make it up to my room and hope that Trix means that she'll come up here. I have more than one reason for that. A lot of it has to do with this ache in my body at seeing her reaction to me.

Remembering that the last time we did something, it was mind-blowing. Part of it also has to do with the fact that I think that there's more to it than either of us is ready to admit. But somehow, I'm not scared about taking that dive the way I normally would.

I sit down on my bed and look at the handiwork that she's done. Other than some stains from the betadine, it looks pretty damn good. For the fact that some of my flesh has been torn off, that is. But the suture work almost looks like a doctor has done it.

I've made the mistake of letting Kratos patch me up before. He's patched a lot of stuff for the club, and while he does the job to save lives, for the most part, his skill is shit. It's never looked good before, and everyone has scars. Not that I give a shit about a scar, but infection, that shit's nasty, and I don't want any part of it.

But the fact that Trix is able to do something like that so calmly and so clean makes me wonder about her. She said she wasn't a doctor, but it makes me realize even more that I know nothing about Trix. We've talked a lot of times, and now we've fucked a lot too. And yet, if someone asks any questions about her personal life, other than being Gemma's roommate, I couldn't tell you anything.

For all I know, she could be the daughter of some kind of a doctor or something, and that's how she knows this.

When I hear her footsteps, my heart reacts, whether I like to admit it or not. It makes me feel like a damn school kid. An adult man, especially an MC member, should not behave this way about some chick, but Trix is different. I just wish I knew how.

She comes inside and immediately locks the door, and not just the door, but the deadbolt.

I stare at it, knowing what it probably means, and it's hard to concentrate after that. I'm kind of fucking glad, though, that she's not going to use my arm as an excuse not to be with me. I guess she trusts her own work.

Trix says nothing, only kicks off her shoes and looks right at me. I stay silent, reading her. I think she's about to say something important, so I better be all fucking years. "When I saw you were hurt, it scared the shit out of me," she admits.

I can't help but smirk. "Guess this means you like me, huh?"

"Shut up, Pan," she tells me. It just makes me smile broader. This is what I like about her and probably also why Kratos immediately had his eye on her. Which threatened me in a weird way. I hadn't defined anything with Trix. Neither of us has said anything about dating other people or dating at all, for that matter, but the way he looked at her, I just can't stand it.

"Why don't you come here and say that to my face, then?" I challenge her.

Trix wasn't playing any games. Instead, she crosses the distance between us. She stands over me and points to my arm. "This is okay, but please don't get hurt worse than this. I just can't . . ." Her voice is quieter, more serious now. She really was fucking scared seeing me with that injury back there.

Shit, our connection is different than I realized. We've got a deep ass connection, and I doubt Trix even realizes it at this point. Between this and the fact that I claimed her downstairs, telling Kratos she was spoken for, and I didn't even give it a second thought . . . It felt totally right for me to say it, but I think this has spiraled way out of leftfield in a way we never expected.

When I met Trix, I liked her. She was beautiful, fun, and cute. I thought she was going to be another bang. Maybe a few times, and then both of us would be done. That's not what this is turning out to be at all.

I grab her ass and pull her close so that her knees hit the bed. I claim her lips, kissing her. "Don't worry. I'm not planning on going anywhere."

Trix looks at me as if trying to figure out if I'm telling her the truth or not. I get the feeling she's been betrayed in some way in life. I think about all the things that she's mentioned to me. The tattoo that turned out to be because she'd been raped before, the fact that she mysteriously knows how to suture a wound at home like that . . . There's definitely something else there under the surface. Just as I had expected. And the fact that she's putting any kind of trust in me with her body or her feelings is something I can't take for granted.

Trix grabs my face and kisses me. Then, she starts pulling my shirt off. I Ignore the slight pain as the shirt scrapes up against the injured arm, knowing she's as gentle as she can be.

My body heats up, and my breath starts coming in jagged waves. No one ever gets me going like this over and over again.

We started to strip, and I couldn't tell you which one of us was pulling what piece of clothing off at that point. It's like a race for both of us to get naked into bed.

Trix helps lay me down carefully, and I favor the side of my body that isn't hurt as I lean toward that side of it. She's not fazed, taking over the work as she kisses and slides down my body. No woman has ever spent this kind of time on me because she feels like she wants to. All the women who have done anything just for me have done it because I paid them to.

This is entirely different, and it makes me feel a little bit vulnerable, which is odd because sex for me is usually the entire opposite.

When she reaches my groin, she teases the area by swirling the little hairs underneath her finger. Who knew something like that would feel so good?

She peeks up at me with hooded eyes, and I practically cum right there. She's so fucking hot, and I don't even think she knows it.

I grunt and grab the bedsheets in my hand. Her tongue nonchalantly begins to slide up and down my sensitive flesh. I hiss and gasp. Her tongue is so warm as she lashes it across me. Then, she reaches the peak, flicks at it with her tongue as pre-cum begins to build, and then places her mouth around me.

I'm seriously about to lose it. "Fuck," I say, grabbing her hair in a large fistful as she begins to work her mouth down my shaft. She takes me deep, swirling her tongue around and changing the pressure from light to hard all the way up and down. She sucks on me a few times, her lips just reminding me of something else and making me want her more.

I just can't decide if I want her to keep going as she is or if I want to yank her up on top of me, my arm be damned.

She's so efficient I start to lose control pretty quickly. My hips are pumping into her involuntarily, and I moan her name.

I fuck her mouth over and over until I'm spilling out inside of her, forcing her to drink me down.

She swallows most of it, some of it spilling down the sides of her mouth as she looks up at me. It's so damn sexy to see me inside of her like that. I don't know what it is about the image, but in my mind, it's worth a million bucks. I kind of wish I had a camera filming us so I could watch this back whenever she's not here and pretend she's sucking on me again.

She wipes at her mouth, and then I motion for her to come to me. She crawls ever so slowly. Her curves and ass make the perfect picture. I use her hair to pull her lips down into me and kiss her before wrapping my good arm around her to pull her up on top of me.

Just looking at her in the position, her breasts, stomach, and that little pink center on full display, gets me hard again.

I like the idea of her being in control this time. "Ride me, baby," I tell her in a husky tone. I can see in the look in her eyes. She's going to obey.

She straddles me and comes up on her knees to position herself.

Her pussy is wet as it slides over the tip of me, waiting to be impaled by my throbbing cock.

I don't think I'll get enough of her tonight to ever be satisfied.

I grab her hips and assist her in lowering onto me and bite my lip as I slide inside. She adjusts to me, wiggling her little ass teasingly with a giggle.

She knows exactly what the fuck she's doing to me.

Then, she begins to bounce on my cock, riding me like an expert cowgirl. She bucks in just the right ways so that she is moaning my name as loudly as I'm moaning hers. If I hadn't already claimed her to Kratos downstairs, he and the rest of the club would know now.

There's no denying what we're doing in here, no matter how well this clubhouse has been built and modified to block out some sound for privacy.

"Shit," I say as her legs begin to quiver, and I know she's close. I pump my hips upward, wanting to have us both cum at the same time to solidify that connection.

I roar as I finish, and she squeezes around me, her breath so heavy that she can't even moan.

I watch her as she comes back down from the high, still slightly rocking her hips until the pleasure has come and gone. After a moment, she slides down next to me and kisses me a few times before trying to get up.

I know what she's doing. She's going to try to cut and run on me. That's not how I want to play it anymore.

I swoop my hand around her waist and pull her back, forcing her to be the little spoon against my chest.

"You're staying. You're worth more than that. Be with me," I growl in her ear. She says nothing at all but stays put after that.

CHAPTER NINE

TRIX

It's the buzzing on my phone that finally gets me out of bed. I'm on my stomach, and I scoot over to the edge of the bed to find my pants for my phone, which is tucked safely inside. I pull it up and see that both text messages are from Gemma.

You stayed over at the club?

Who are you banging?

"Shit," I say out loud, rolling over on my back and huffing. I know that what Pan and I have been doing has been going on long enough that it's not just going to end up being a fling. I'm not going to have a choice but to tell Gemma.

I hate keeping secrets, but that doesn't mean that I'm looking forward to doing so either. If we had just talked a couple of times and I got the man out of my system, and I told her, she probably wouldn't make a big deal about it, but that's not the case here.

I must have woken Pan up because he starts to stir next to me, rolling over to give me a smile.

I quickly type a text back to Gemma.

I'll tell you when I get home. We need to talk.

Great, now she's going to be blowing up my phone until I do get there, but I can't just leave Pan hanging after last night. He made me stay. He told me that I was worth something and that I shouldn't just run off. He ended up holding me all night.

That is until whenever I decided to kick the covers off and turn over onto my stomach, which is typical for me at night. He seems to have put up with it well, though.

A groggy Pan leans over and gives me a kiss on my bare shoulder. "Go back to sleep. We've got all the time in the world, right?" Pan asks. It sounds extremely appealing, but I couldn't sleep right now if I wanted to. And I don't because I have to go talk to Gemma no matter how much I'm dreading it before I pussy out of it.

I sigh again and turn to look at him. "Wow, you're stressed about something. What is it? I mean, I can help with that." Pan winks, pressing himself up against my thigh. I look down at his impressive morning wood and give a crooked grin and then laugh. But it doesn't sound real.

"Gemma noticed I didn't come home last night. And she knows that I was here. At the club."

"And?" Pan scratches his head in confusion. I chalk it up to the fact that the guy just woke up.

"She knows what it means. She knows it means I'm fucking somebody. She said so herself, and she expects me to come home and tell her all about it. I can't keep this from her anymore anyway. Not after last night. So, I'm stressed about having to tell Gemma that I've been screwing her brother and plan on continuing to."

Pan grabs my ass at that and kisses me on the lips. It's more of a smack. "Gemma won't care."

I look him right in the eyes. "You know for a fucking fact that Gemma is a drama queen. We're not just talking about something casual here anymore. We've done this a lot, and like I said, I don't plan on stopping. Unless you do. In which case, I guess this is irrelevant?" I go to move, but he pulls me back.

"Of course, she's going to care," I add

He begins to cackle. "It doesn't mean shit. Everything is fine. It's not something to worry about. You're one of her best friends and her roommate. I'm her brother. How long could she possibly stay angry at us? She has to face us every day."

He's much more relaxed about it than I expected him to be. I figure he wouldn't want his baby sister in his business or some shit like that. I certainly wish that I could think like that, but a small part of me wonders if maybe I'm so pessimistic about it all because my life as a kid was less than ideal if I'm putting it nicely.

Nothing has ever worked out well for me. Gemma and all the girls are my bright spot. And I'm not knocking on Pan, he's been a bright spot lately, too, but they are my family. I can't lose them. I'm afraid one wrong move and I will, and I'll be back to square one all over again.

But maybe that unlucky streak is broken. I got out of it, and here I am, a thriving adult. I have a hot guy next to me that I really like. And he cuddled me all night. It can't be that bad, right?

Maybe Pan's right. Only time will tell.

"I see those gears moving. You know I'm right, don't you?" Pan asks happily. The shit-eating grin on his face is because he's proud of himself for being right about something.

I roll my eyes, but I'm sobered quickly by him pulling me close. He kisses me so intensely I almost fall off the bed.

His tongue slides into my mouth and starts to carve out every crevice and inch of my gums and teeth. He's tasting all of me, and I begin to wonder what his tongue would be like somewhere else.

I know I'm getting sucked back into him, and I don't even care right now. I can spare time for a little bit more, and then I can go to my doom and tell Gemma what I've been doing.

Pan rolls on top of me, throwing caution to the wind about his arm. I watch the stitches nervously for a moment, but then he is down at my lips again. He begins to nibble and suck at my bottom lip, causing my whole body to grow warm. He feels amazing like this, and he's hovering over me, his warmth touching every spot on my body. I want him all over again.

Then, he rips his lips away from me, and I'm left whimpering. But then he picks back up at my neck, sucking and biting while moving down toward my chest, my stomach. I think I'm going to have a stroke from the pleasure. My whole body is on fire.

He works a trail from one hip to the other, back and forth, showing me exactly what he can do with his tongue. I might just get to find out. I'm aching with anticipation, and I grab the bedsheets to try to keep from just shoving him down. Finally, he licks down, right across my groin, and then finds my clit flicking it back and forth.

I gasp, taking a shaky breath or two as he continues to desensitize me a little bit to the feeling so that it's not both agony and pleasure at the same time. I bring my knees up and spread my legs wider for him, my hips bucking automatically against him.

His tongue slides down further, finding my center. He slides himself inside and begins to lap me up like I have some life-saving milk and honey or something. I arch my back in response, Pan finding the sensitive flesh inside and starting to press into it. My hand falls on his head automatically, my hand holding his head there. I don't want him to stop, and I moan to let him know it.

I started to wish it was something else inside of me. I start to beg, "Please, Pan." I ask him quietly at first and then get louder, "Please, I want you inside of me."

He simply looks up for a moment, and I can tell he has no intention of rushing this at all. I squirm under him as he begins to lap me up once more, licking me up and down and flicking my clit once more. He always pauses every few minutes to make sure that I'm in complete agony and torture.

Pan darts his tongue in and out vigorously, and I have lost all control of my mouth and my mind. I buck into him viciously, and finally, I'm shaking, shivering, as I have pulse after pulse wracking me.

Just when I think that I can't handle it anymore, he climbs on top of me. In one fell swoop, he slides inside, filling me up instantly. I let out a scream that probably alerts the entire club yet again to what we're doing up here. I guess it's a good thing I'm going to tell Gemma because if I don't, someone else will at this point.

His thrusts get a rhythm going, and he gets up on his knees, his hands on mine. He goes hard and deep the whole time, holding my gaze. I don't think I've ever had a man do that for me before.

My experience with sex has been all over the place. When I was young, it was very bad. I was able to kind of get out of it, but I don't think I've ever had someone make me feel this safe and this good at the same time. Pan is just the right amount of sweet and wild.

I thrust my own hips up to meet him as I get close, my legs turning to jelly as I cum all over again.

As he moves off me, he looks at me and asks, "Are you at least a little bit less stressed now?"

I break out in full laughter. That's another thing. He always knows how to lighten the mood. "Yes, I am."

"Seriously though, don't be too worried. No matter what, everything is going to be fine." His tone has turned serious, and his hand slides up and down my arm to reassure me. He has to be right. It's going to be okay.

I get out of bed and stand up, and I know it's late morning. I begin searching for wherever the hell my bra and my shirt went, and I see a strap tucked up under the bed at the bottom edge. As I bend over to pick it up, I hear Pan as he sits up in the bed. "Hey, where did you get those scars on the back of your legs?"

About an inch or so below my ass, I have scars running up and down the backs of my thighs. I knew he would see them at some point, but I had been thinking so much about Gemma that I forgot he might see them this morning now that it's light outside.

I don't know if I'm ready for that, and I freeze. Instantly, the memories come flooding back.

PTSD is a bitch that hangs over you your entire life. At any given moment, it can all come back and haunt you and re-traumatize you, even if you're years out of it. Even if you think you're fully healed.

In my mind, I'm tied up to a wooden crucifix. Instead of facing outward like Jesus, though, my ass is facing out. I have to turn my cheek to the right so that my mouth and nose do not smash into it. I'm 18 years old, and I know what's coming could easily kill me. And if it doesn't, it will break me forever.

I've had these things happening to me since I was younger. This forsaken shithole of an orphanage is a joke. How many of them get away with this kind of treatment of children, I don't know, and I don't really give a fuck. What I care about is the fact that I'm aging out.

Two hours from now, I'm officially 18 years old. Because I was born at 2:20 a.m., according to my birth certificate. And that means tomorrow morning I'm getting bussed out of here. I'm no longer allowed to stay here because I age out of the system.

But this place is not going to let me go before one more punishment, and it's going to be the punishment to end all punishments.

"Congratulations, you're going out into the world. You won't get to tempt all of us with your unholy body anymore," the priest says. I don't even remember this one's name only because I've blocked it out. They're in and out as well as some of the nuns who always

keep themselves quiet. Probably because they're afraid it'll happen to them too, and then it'll ruin their positions as nuns.

But this fucker, he's the ringleader. He's the one who runs the show. Who lets the other men in and handles discipline. I refuse to humanize him by remembering a name because, to me, he's just a monster.

I can hear the whip in his hand as he uses it to intimidate me. I've been hit with it before. It's a bullwhip, and it hurts like hell.

I've only ever been hit once or twice at once, but I get the feeling that this time I'm going to walk out of here, no crawl out of here, with thick scars and ripped, infected wounds probably all over my body.

I don't dare say anything back to him. I've done that before, and I've regretted it. I used to stick up for myself and say that I wasn't a sinner, that I couldn't help the way that I looked. I even used to try to make myself ugly. I got a hold of a pair of scissors once and chopped my hair off. I did such a botched job that the nuns had to shave it almost bald.

I only got made fun of and beat for the fact that I then looked like a boy, which was wrong in God's eyes. They said I must have been a dike or something. I was just trying to get eyes off of myself. I was trying to get them to stop calling me a temptress, whore, harlot. All of those words dug into me, and I began to believe them.

I tune out his words, knowing the kind of vitriol he's going to spew. I'm going to have to if I'm going to survive the rest of this. I take a deep breath and hold it as the whip cracks.

"1," I count in my head, and then I take another deep breath and hold it.

The whip cracks again and hits just below the first mark.

"2," I say to myself.

Tears are streaming from my eyes to the point that I can't see, and I'm ready to just let go and die by the time I count to six, and he's not done yet.

At eight, I hang limply from the cross, and he finally puts the whip down. He tells me all kinds of things as he comes up to me, about how I've always tempted him. How even now, with the screams I'm making, that I'm moaning for him, begging for him to commit sexual sins against God. "If it's not me doing it, it'll be somebody else, so you better get used to it since you're going out into the world now, you little whore," he tells me in my ear.

Between the pain and then the feeling of him as he shoves himself inside me, I puke all over the cross and down toward my feet. It doesn't stop him. He just smacks me on my cheek and keeps going harder.

I come back to reality and turn around to look at Pan. I probably look like I've seen a ghost. And I guess it is the ghost of me. "My past isn't filled with happiness. It was rough, and my scars are mementos that tell everyone I literally endured hell on earth."

It's the best answer I can give him right now. I know he's not going to judge me for it, especially in his line of work, but I'm just too triggered right now. Luckily, he doesn't press, and I respect that about him.

I finish getting dressed, and as I do, he gets up to get dressed as well. "You need a ride?" he asks, and I realize that I do.

"Yeah, I guess so. I came with Calli, and of course, she's not here so . . . if you wouldn't mind?"

"And miss a chance to have you holding on to me on the back of my bike? Of course, I'll take you home."

His warm smile makes me feel better again, and I follow him out to his bike. We climb on, and I feel like something really is starting when I wrap my arms around him. This is what safety feels like.

When we get to my house, I stare up at the door and stop. I'd much rather stay with Pan, but I know if I don't go in, we're going to get caught before I can even talk to Gemma about it. "Let me know how it goes, okay?" he says quietly. I nod and head inside. "Let's do this," I say to myself.

CHAPTER TEN

I watch Trix for another minute as she gets dressed, looking over the scars and wondering when and how she could have gotten them. I leave it alone, though, because it's none of my fucking business right now. Hopefully, she'll tell me one day, but I don't need to know right now.

I get up and get dressed and offer her a ride. She lets me know that Calli is the one who brought her yesterday, which is what I figured. She has no other way home than me. I am ecstatic about the fact that I get to take her on the back of my bike. I get to drop her off at home. It feels surreal.

My giddiness is absolutely fucking ridiculous, and I know that if the guys catch me acting like this, I'm going to get razzed. But she's worth being razzed over, that's for sure. Besides, Eros has gotten his fair share of razzing from me already over Calli, so I guess it's my damn turn anyway.

Right before we walk out the door, I pull up my phone. I shoot out a text message to all of the officers and Eros letting them know I'm going to be taking Trixie home. There's a lot of shit going on right now, obviously, with the Serpents and the fact that I have an injury. They're gonna get worried if I don't tell them this time.

"Okay, babe, let's go." We head to the parking lot, and I savor every moment as we both mount the bike, and she wraps her arms around me. I go as slow as I can get away with, cruising and enjoying the feel of her behind me and the wind in our hair as we go down the street.

When I pull up in front of the house, I can feel the tension again. She's so damn worried about Gemma, and I just don't want her to be. Gemma may be a drama queen, but she loves people unconditionally. That includes her friends, and Trix has been her friend for a while now. She's not just going to shun her over this, even if it pisses her the fuck off.

She gets off and starts to walk away after I tell her not to worry, but then I grab her hand for a moment. "Thank you for trusting me enough to tell me a little bit about your past. That can't have been easy," I tell her. "Whenever you're ready, I'll be here to listen to the rest of it. No pressure, okay?"

Trix gives a sweet and soft smile and then walks away again. I lean against my bike and wait for her to get inside, just to make sure she's safe, and then I pull my phone out again to check my texts. Zeus sent a message to everyone earlier today. He's calling church. I wonder what the hell he's learned since our little visit to the farm that led to the deaths of several of our enemies.

I guess there's nothing better than to get information that we need coming out of the woodworks than a mass death that you can't ignore.

I hop back on my bike and immediately head back to the clubhouse. I go straight into church, and I realize I'm the last one there. Zeus gives me a hard look, and then I take my place next to Eros.

"What the fuck happened with the Vile Serpents?" he asks, trying to meet the eyes of every single one of us. I have no idea what the fuck he's talking about. As far as the bullets flying back and forth, he knows all about that. And he knows about my injury since Calli told him.

When all Zeus gets is silence, he says, "There are reports about Thorn hassling yet another woman the same way he was doing to my daughter. So, tell me, what the hell is going on, and where is Thorn? Why wasn't he there?"

No one says anything; everyone looks at each other with their hands in their pockets. The thing is, we all know nothing about Thorn. We didn't know if he was staying there or not, as well as some of his officers. We just knew that everyone that was there that day died.

Hades clears his throat. "I told you, boss, we don't know anything. We tried to grab the last asshole standing, but he offed himself before we could get any information out of him. Specifically said he was doing it to keep information from us because Thorn would do much worse than death or some shit like that."

Zeus gives Hades a look for speaking out of turn like that, and if looks could kill, this one has Hades by the balls. However, Zeus doesn't say anything else about that.

Hades was right, none of us knew anything, and Zeus realized it. "So, no one knows shit about it. Well, that's just fucking great." He raises his voice even louder, and it's clear he's about to lose his shit. I can't exactly blame him. Had he been there, he would have torn that fucker who killed himself limb from limb afterward just to set an example and found a way to save the pieces to hand to Thorn once we find him.

Eros raises his hand, and Zeus acknowledges him. "Well, I can look into it. I'll see what I can find out about this girl he's harassing and where this one has been seen. He can't get too damn far without his MC. He's crippled without them. You know that fucker never fights his own battles. Not alone."

Zeus nods. "Thanks, and Pan, you're assigned with him."

"Yes, Prez," I say.

Zeus continues, "Now, Hermes, I need a fucking update about people getting the dope back on the streets. And how are the books looking?" He moves on with the rest of the meeting. I wonder why he's bringing this up now after he's been fuming about the Thorn situation. I get that it's important to be making a profit, but I wonder why this is so pressing right now.

"We're not doing bad at all, but there's been a 3% drop in sales," Hermes answers.

Zeus grits his teeth and begins to pace back and forth. It can't be a coincidence. I remember when we caught that member of the Serpents selling in our territory before. "Kratos, Cronos, Dion, you're gonna figure out what the fucking problem is, do you understand me?"

"It's got to be Thorn. Not too long ago, we caught the Vile Serpents' people selling dope to a teenager or trying to before we beat the shit out of him for it. They were doing it in our damn territory. I bet they're involved somehow. They're stealing clientele or something."

Zeus agrees. "Alright, everybody, thank you for coming. You can go but keep an eye out for this shit and tell me if you see anything at all that could be related." We all give a grunt of agreement, and then church is dismissed.

CHAPTER ELEVEN

When I get into the house, the vibe is strange. Gemma's just standing in the living room. Her eyes are entirely blank. I instantly wonder if she's realized that it's Pan who brought me home.

Fuck, I'm sure as soon as she heard the engine of a bike pull up, she just looked out the window and saw who the hell it was. We didn't kiss or anything, but that doesn't mean she didn't put two and two together after all the time we spent together before.

With a stoic blank stare, she says, "I should have seen it. I should have seen you were getting together with my brother." She's clearly upset, but it's not anger. It's shock. Which doesn't make any fucking sense considering she's caught us flirting several times and said something about it.

Up until now, all of it's been mostly teasing from her. And I knew she would react badly, but not like this. And not before I even got a chance to speak my peace.

Gemma turns to the side to look me dead on. Her eyes meet mine, and then she blinks a few times as if she's trying to blink the shock away. She runs her hands through her bright, Irish red, curly hair and says, "My brother? Of all the guys there, you're fucking my brother?"

What the hell was going on with her? I just don't understand the reaction at all. I expect her to be mad. To yell at me. But this? I don't get it. But I don't dare say anything about it right now either. I just listen, hoping she can get it out and we can fix this. And maybe she'll let me talk later, let me explain that it's gonna be fine.

"Here's the thing," Gemma says, "the girls in this house are like my sisters. You're always going to be involved in my life. All of you. So, what the hell happens if my brother totally destroys your heart. Will that mean the end of our friendship then?"

This is what she's worried about? She thinks I'll blame her, or I'll distance myself from her if Pan and I break up? I don't ever think of Gemma as being an insecure person, but maybe this is her weakness, and I just haven't seen it yet because we've all been so close, and we've never stepped on each other's toes like this.

I open my mouth to say something, but she beats me to the punch.

"Probably, right?!" Tears start running down Gemma's face, and I try to temper my frustration. I don't understand why she's feeling this way in particular or why she's interrupting me, not letting me speak. That part pisses me off, but she is allowed to have feelings. And they're totally valid.

Gemma is afraid. She's afraid of losing me. And that should mean something to me if she would just calm down. I could solve this easily.

"Look, Gemma, we're all entitled to our feelings, but—" Gemma is muttering to herself, pacing back and forth. Calli comes into the room and walks straight through the living area to see what's going on. She pauses, surveying the tension in the room.

Gemma turns on her instantly, "Calli, did you know Trix was fucking my brother?"

Calli looks incredibly uncomfortable having walked into this. And I don't like that she's becoming the middle person here. "I kind of assumed that they were, that that might be happening." She doesn't lie, but she doesn't rat me out either. I appreciate that and give her a nod behind Gemma's back. Gemma needs to chill the fuck out, or this is what's gonna make her lose all of us.

"And so what, Gemma? If they're happy, then that's all that matters." I appreciate that Calli is trying to diffuse the situation, but I know that those words are probably going to blow Gemma up further. I've known her a little bit longer and telling her that she feels wrong about something is about the worst fucking thing you can do.

Gemma scoffs. "My brother goes through women like he does with bikes. He changes every couple of months. Or possibly flavor of the week. Why would Trix be any different?"

The suggestion that I might not mean anything at all to Pan is kind of insulting. Right now, I would just rather go hide in the bedroom, but unfortunately, it's a bedroom we share. That doesn't mean I can't go get some privacy in there for a bit so that Gemma can hang out with Calli or something. I'll go read a damn book or something. But I know it's rude to walk away before there's some kind of solution here.

"I don't want you to be something else that my brother just throws away. And I don't want to be resented for the actions of my brother either." Gemma turns to me, some of the tears drying up. At least she's not yelling and screaming anymore or crying.

I take a step toward her. "Gemma, I will never resent you if something goes down between the two of us. It wouldn't be your fault. It's never been your fault if your brother behaves a certain way. You know me. Why would I blame it on you?"

Gemma scoffs and throws her hands up in the air, clearly not buying it. This isn't going well, so I just breeze past her and go to the bedroom. I lay down on the bed and pull my phone out. Pan should at least know that this isn't going like I thought or like he thought.

She knows. Didn't go well.

That says enough for now, in my opinion. He can ask me about it later.

I lay there, staring at the ceiling and knowing that that's not going to get me anywhere. The stress is just building up and causing a lot of pain in my body. This is not a good way to be, so I decided instead to take a hot shower to get the stress out of my body. Then, I go ahead and head up to the kitchen to see if it's clear.

Luckily, I'm the only one in here now, and I can make the birthday cake that's due next week in peace.

Honestly, the argument is still sitting at the back of my mind. What if all this stuff with Pan is not even worth it? I mean, I could lose my best friend and my roommate over it. I don't want to fight with her. I don't want to fight with anyone. I want my chosen family to stay that way. Are great sex and the way he's been nice to me really enough to put a wrecking ball through this? I just don't know.

CHAPTER TWELVE

PAN

I'm lounging in my bed when I get yet another text from my sister. I simply laugh and shake my head. Her texts over the past few days have been increasingly hostile, but nothing I can't handle. And other than that, it's been pretty quiet around the club. Which is actually kind of boring and concerning, considering it means I haven't heard from Trix, and we haven't figured out what the hell is going on with the war either.

My phone vibrates again.

Ignoring me doesn't make you any less of a shithead.

Love you too, sis.

I figure if I kill her with kindness, then maybe she'll shut up about it. If she's giving me this kind of flak, I can't imagine what Trix is going through inside of the house with her, and I'm kind of worried that that's why I haven't heard from her.

If Gemma has ruined what we have before it even gets started, she's never gonna hear the fucking end of it from me. I'm going to shove it in her face the rest of her damn life and be there to wreck her next relationship too.

I tell myself it's like water washing over my shoulders, nothing to be upset about. Her words, they really aren't anything to be upset about. I'm mostly upset about not hearing from Trix. I hope she's okay.

Literally, the last I heard from her was just her letting me know that things were not going well with Gemma. Which I should have fucking expected. I had sat here like a douche bag and told Trix over and over that it was going to be okay, that Gemma was just going to be a drama queen for a minute, and she'd get over it because she loves Trixie, and she loves me.

Apparently, I underestimated her ability to hold a grudge against me.

With nothing else to do, I head downstairs to the club and see that Calli's here. She's sitting on Eros' lap as they watch Hades and Hermes play a game of pool with each other. Zeus is lounging across from them. If anyone is going to be able to tell me anything about Trixie, it's going to be Calli.

I go up to them and greet Eros before I turn to Calli. "Have you seen Trix?" I ask. The look on her face and the fact that she immediately clams up tells me my answer before I even hear her say anything.

"I have." I look at her in annoyance. That means she knows why I'm asking. I hate the girl code. "Trix has been busy working on a lot of cake orders over the last few days, to be fair." I just nod and go along with it at this point.

"Calli, was she at the house when you left to come here?" I ask her.

Calli squints her eyes at me in annoyance. "Yes, but if she asks, you didn't hear shit from me. I'm not going to be the one responsible for whatever the hell you do next." I smile at her sass, but I know that I owe her one.

I'm going to turn this shit around right here and now. I'm not going to wait another day to hear from Trix. She's going to be hearing from me instead.

"Noted," I assure her. I go back upstairs to my room and start looking through my clothes. I find one of my favorite shirts and sniff it. Thank goodness it smells pretty damn clean. Tomorrow's laundry day, so I'm a little lacking right now.

It's a Warped Tour t-shirt. The only time I ever went. I actually got it signed by Bert McCracken, and if I told Trix, she'd probably get a kick out of it, but the guy kissed me on the lips. He's outrageous. But in the best damn way.

I pull it over my head and exchange my jeans and boxers for fresh pairs. Finally, I slip my shoes on and then head out the door. When I straddle my bike, I pull out my phone. I pull up the local pizza place and decide to order takeout pizza to be delivered to her house. It will be a good surprise. Hopefully, she likes pepperoni.

I race out, wanting to beat the pizza there. I don't want a surprise pizza showing up at her door and then her being like, what the fuck. She needs me to go along with it.

I get there with 10 minutes to spare and don't even bother knocking. If I do, there's a chance that if Gemma is home, she would likely be the one answering the door, and then she would just slam the door in my face. Which will give Trix a chance to say that she doesn't want to talk to me since she probably feels bad about whatever is going on with Gemma.

When I get inside and turn the corner, I can see Trix is in the kitchen. She's doing something with the fondant, which I should expect considering her life at this point is pretty much cupcakes and cakes for many occasions. It's how she makes her money.

She bakes for the clubhouse now too, and Zeus has fallen in love with her baking. She doesn't see me yet, and she's dancing around the kitchen to Dorothy, one of my favorite bands as well.

I get closer, and I turn off the Bluetooth speaker. "Dorothy's voice is sick," I comment, leaning up against the counter. Trix jumps and then turns around.

"What the hell are you doing here?"

"Can't a man come over and see how his favorite lady is doing?" I'm rewarded with a brilliant smile just like I'd hoped.

Gemma comes from the living room and says, "Barf." I look at her, frustrated at this point. I guess she's still annoyed, and she doesn't really wanna see this, but it's getting out of hand for the fact that we're all adults, and I don't need Trix to have this energy right now. I know she's probably taking on a lot of extra jobs the past few days to avoid me but also to avoid the stress. She seems to be real high strung with this stuff. I don't need Gemma to continue to pile this shit on her.

"Suck it up, Gemma, 'cause I really like Trix, and I wanna see where this goes."

I look back at Trix, whose eyes are now beaming with positivity, which isn't exactly something that normally happens with her. She usually seems to be really in her head about everything, and I'm glad to see that she's happy right now. And I did that. Why would I want to ruin that?

"Do you want some dessert?" Trix asks out of the blue. Gemma stomps away, back to the living room, and plops down on the couch, deflated since she's not having any effect on us right now. "Someone actually canceled an order last minute and then demanded their deposit back, so now we have cake."

Who am I to turn that shit down? "Hell yeah, let's see it."

Trix smiles, showing her perfect white teeth, and then goes to the fridge and pulls out the cake. I start cracking the hell up. Before me is what appears to be a cake that doesn't look like a cake at all. It's a wide-open, spread-eagle vagina.

Taking a closer look, it's even worse. It's bloody with a baby's head poking out.

"Is this a fucking joke?" I ask her. She starts laughing too but then shakes her head.

"No, it's a push cake. Like for a baby shower."

I look at the thing again and can't believe some poor, unsuspecting woman was about to have to eat a cake that looks like that when she's about to give birth herself. If I were a woman, that would traumatize me forever and never make me want to give birth, which would be a real problem with a baby currently growing in my belly. What were they thinking?

It's probably best that it was canceled, but I'm not so sure about eating it.

I scoff. "That shit looks so real," I tell her. It's the truth. You'd never know it was a cake without someone telling you. It looks more like a mannequin, like what they use to teach doctors how to operate.

"Thanks for the compliment," Trix says. "It means I did my job perfectly. If only the client had gotten to see that."

"Yeah, but with it looking that real, I'm not sure I could eat it," I admit to her.

Trix goes into the drawer and pulls out a large knife, and then drives it straight down into the vagina slicing cleanly through it.

"Holy fuck," I grimace.

She pulls a small piece out. "Look, it's just vanilla cake with buttercream icing, and it's delicious." She takes a bite, leaving a bit of icing at the corner of her mouth, which is so damn cute.

With no regard for Gemma at all, I lean in and lick it right off. "Mmmm, it is pretty damn good." I swallow, then kiss her again.

The doorbell rings, letting me know the pizza has arrived.

"What's going on?" Trix motions toward the door.

"I got pizza, of course. It's a mandatory date night," I tell her. "And apparently, this date includes eating out a pussy together."

She cracks up at that.

CHAPTER THIRTEEN

The pizza is excellent. I know a lot of girls wouldn't touch the shit because of the calories, but I can't live without pizza and cake. It's just not possible. I can make up for it in other ways. I mean, I eat pretty damn healthy otherwise.

I'm on my second piece of cake, a tequila on the rocks that Pan made for me, sitting on the coffee table as we talk about some of our interests. I've just asked him about superheroes and am shocked at his answer.

"Seriously, DC!?" I squeak at him, slapping my knee. "I can't believe that. What the fuck? I totally pegged you for like a Captain America or Iron man type."

He takes a sip of his own drink and screws up his face in disgust. "Those assholes are so holier than thou. See, it's Batman I like. He knows his life is dangerous, and so is he. He knows he's shitty on both sides—the billionaire one's too high and mighty for his own good and the vigilante delivering justice at any cost, emotions always making him go way too far," Pan explains.

"Wow, sounds like that man crush runs super deep," I tease.

He just rolls his eyes. "Have you seen how he is with the ladies?" Pan wiggles his eyebrow, and I just lose it, almost spitting tequila all over us both.

"You did not just say that shit."

"Oh, I definitely did."

"Hmm, I don't know about Batman, but Robin can be kind of sexy," I tell him, licking my lips.

He clambers for words for a moment which is totally cute, and then says, "Maybe it's something we'll have to play with sometime. Robin can save a good damsel in distress."

"Lord knows I need saving," I mumble to myself.

"So," I say, clapping my hands and changing the subject, "tell me something else real about you. Maybe like your most embarrassing moment or how many girls you've dated."

He chuckles. "Unless you count middle school, I haven't dated a whole lot of anyone. I wasn't looking for anyone too serious when I was young, as I probably was right not to do. I didn't have the maturity to handle it. Most guys just don't."

I nod along. I can totally respect that.

"As an adult, I don't know. The MC environment makes it easy to get needs met without having to wrap them up in a neat little bow and commit. It's not that I don't want to. I'm just not looking to point fingers and pick anyone just because I think it would be convenient to have someone around. I want a real connection."

He meets my eyes, and I bite my lip, suddenly feeling nervous.

"Want to put on some music?" I finally ask.

"Yes. I loved what you were listening to earlier. You can learn so much about a person from their taste in music."

I log in to Spotify and hand him my phone. "Surprise me with a playlist of stuff you like," I tell him.

He doesn't hesitate, and before I know it, we're jamming to a strange mix of modern indie rock and 90s R&B.

A couple of glasses of tequila in, and I become an open book. Pan and I have had an excellent day, really. He's kept me laughing throughout the night, and I'd almost completely forgotten about the fact that Gemma basically hates me for the fact that I'm dating her brother since she'd decided to leave us alone once we moved to the living room.

Well, not dating. We haven't exactly defined it, but it feels like that's what's going on. That's not the way Gemma sees it, though, which is entirely the problem. She still thinks that to him, I'm just another notch on his bedpost. If I'm going to put myself all in and really enjoy it, I can't worry about that kind of thing, though.

"I like that you're opening up to me. I feel like I should know more about you, and I just don't," Pan expresses to me. I'm slowly sipping at some vodka now, trying not to get so drunk that I'm not going to be able to perform later because Pan is looking real sexy tonight, especially after what he did for me. Showing up here and surprising me with pizza and a date night.

It's a real sweet thing and something no one's ever really done for me. Especially when we've been having some kind of problems. He could have just ghosted me.

"Honestly, there's not really much worth knowing. I don't mean that in like a little self-esteem kind of way. It's just I don't have a lot of good or interesting things to tell you," I admit to him.

He shakes his head and takes a swig of a beer that I got him just a few moments ago. "You don't have to feel obligated to tell me anything if you don't want, but I promise that's probably much more interesting to me than you think."

"Well, if you're ready to get into that drama, I don't know who my parents are. I literally have no idea at all. I was actually dropped off at a fire station when I was a baby." I find myself laughing. It's kind of darkly funny. It's dumb that I can't connect to any family members from my past. That I'm literally alone and have no one, simply from being dropped off at a fire station. Like things were that bad. And a lot of people would say, *'well, at least it wasn't a dumpster'*, but the result was still the same.

Pan gives grace like always. I can't imagine why Gemma has such a bad viewpoint of him. Judging a man by how he treats his flings is not really accurate or fair. Especially if those flings know that that's how they are. But then again, she could be right, and I could be headed for a complete and utter heart-shattering destruction. Only time will tell, right?

"So, obviously, I ended up in the foster care system. Nobody came to adopt me. I don't know why. I was always being told that a pretty little girl like me with not really any health problems would find a family without an issue. But really, we were full up. I eventually ended up at an orphanage."

"Damn," Pan comments, shaking his head. He takes the last swig of his beer and then sets the bottle down on the table with a clink. "I'm sorry for that, though, 'cause that shit sounds rough. We definitely have people in the MC I'm sure you could relate to."

I down the rest of my vodka because I'm going to need some courage for this, but Pan has been so good to me that I feel like I can totally open up to him. It means a lot to me, plus once I start spilling, it's hard to stop.

"Unfortunately, it gets worse from there. See that orphanage, it was filled with a bunch of awful men who enjoyed molesting and raping the girls there." We lock eyes for a moment, and I see his face. He's thinking about the scars on me. He's thinking about the tattoo that he found that I have and the reason why I had been so hesitant to talk about them.

I can't say he's the first one to ever give me that look. I don't seem like that type of girl on the outside. In fact, I've worked really hard to not just be *that* girl.

Despite the fact that I have ongoing PTSD from everything that was done to me, I've done a lot of work and know that I don't need to blame myself or wallow in my misery. I've been really well put together ever since I got out.

Everyone seems to see this pretty face. A young woman with a talent who's got things all together, unlike a lot of her peers. But the only reason I have it together is because I had to. I had to have it together to survive. And that kind of shit still hurts even if I don't show it.

I look down at the ground and say, "The women weren't much better, but at least they only beat us or starved us." I shrug as if it's no big deal, even though I know it is. Sometimes it helps to minimize it. It makes the pain not so real.

"That's not better, not by a long shot. It's fucking foul." I can't exactly disagree with him. He's right, but I don't really have a choice. I push back a lot of my pain so that I can move on in life. I think Pan sees it. He hears it in my silence.

He looks at me, holding my face in his gaze until I finally am forced to look at him in the eyes again. "Wait, were you sexually assaulted while you were there at this orphanage?"

I feel no need to hesitate. It's not my damn fault, even though it still eats me up at night. "Yes. From the age of 14, all the way up to the day that I turned 18. The place was supposed to be a Christian orphanage. There were actually pastors that would come in to talk to the kids. Several of them paid special attention to the young girls. They liked to punish the pretty ones for tempting them."

As I try to describe the horrors that I went through without being too incredibly graphic to Pan, Pan pulls me against him.

He pulls me against his chest, kissing my forehead and then letting me lean on him. "You're safe. You're safe with me," he tells me, rubbing my back in a soothing way. This is all I ever needed before. Why has it been so hard to get?

But of course, the way he's being so kind causes all the feelings to come to the surface. They're bubbling up fast.

Some of these feelings I didn't even know I had at all, and some of them I thought I had buried deep or gotten rid of entirely. It goes to show that trauma just likes to keep coming back like a boomerang. The scars are constantly being ripped open and being forced to heal again.

I start to cry, surprising myself. It's not something I've cried about in a long time. Part of me, I guess, is still that helpless little girl who was abused for the first time. The whole time, no matter how many sobs there are and no matter how much of the story I get out between the sobs, Pan just holds me there.

He's constantly reassuring me that it's okay and he's here to listen. Pan definitely isn't what Gemma thinks he is. I don't get it at all. Pan is a great man. I never thought I'd be with a great man like this. I like the way that he cares for me and the way he wants to make me feel safe.

I guess it's one good part of being in an MC is learning to be protective. That's what they all do, even if I have my qualms about it.

I pull back a little and wipe my tears, sniffling a bit. I can't imagine what I look like right now, but I don't worry so much about the mascara or eyeliner dripping. With so many emotions flooding through me right now, there's only one thing I can do. I lock my lips with Pan's. All of my passion, gratefulness, and feelings are being put into that kiss.

I turn my head to the side as our mouths open to each other. I press my body up against his, our mouths attacking each other like we need each other's breath to survive.

This time it's different. I feel it from his side too. It's beautiful and caring. I think I have real feelings for Pan, and I think he has them for me too. Whatever this thing is, I'm ready for it.

I don't know why I was so worried before about it being worth it. Feelings like this and someone who takes care of me like this are worth more than anything, and eventually, Gemma will see it too. It will be okay.

I slide down my sweats as Pan pulls me into his lap. His hands are gentle with me as he continues to stroke my back after taking my shirt off. His touch is so tender and yet sensual, and it drives me crazy. He looks me in the eyes, and I practically start crying again from what I see there.

He feels the connection, too, something beyond what we thought when we first had a crush on each other. When we first had sex, it's grown this way so fast. It makes me wonder where we'll be weeks from now or months from now.

I reach between us to unzip his pants and pull them down a little, along with his boxers. He's already hard for me, but as he helps me slide on, it's slow and sensual.

I rock my hips just slightly on him, and his hands are everywhere. But it's more like he's taking his time in exploring me. Making a mental map of all of my body's curves, rolls, and flaws. He's exploring every inch of me. And when he's done with his hands, he does it with his tongue. It lashes up against my neck and my collarbone, tracing the delicate lines of my physique.

As good as my center feels with him inside of me, the way we're being attentive to each other is even more special. It feels even better, like a braingasm. This is so different than our other encounters like a shift is definitely happening with us.

His hands slip around my ass cheeks as I thrust back and forth, up and down on him. I'm in no hurry.

When my insides start to grip tightly around him, about to reach the peak of pleasure, his mouth is on mine again, and I would usually find it odd and vulnerable, but our eyes are open as we kiss, watching each other's reactions. It's like we don't want to miss a moment of what's going on.

I rock myself to the climax, moaning into his mouth and sharing his breaths. As I shiver above him and cum, he holds me there with his eyes and with his hands. Then, he begins to pull me in a little harder over him, using my hips to finish himself off. Finally, he's grunting and moaning to the feel of himself inside me.

I kiss him, coaxing him to cum for me, and he does. Then, I lay down, and we make love all over again.

Afterward, while he's holding me and kissing my ear softly, I drift off to sleep. He asks, "Are you coming to the Christmas party? We host it every year for club and family."

Family? Is he referring to me as family?

"I'd love to come, though I don't know what to get you."

"I'm sure you'll think of something," he teases, nipping at my ear. I laugh softly and nod.

"Yeah, I'm sure I will. I know you liked that pussy cake," I joke, and he tickles my side. "Goodnight," I tell him.

"Night, Trix."

One Week Later

"Well, ladies, we've done good," Calli says as we all step into the clubhouse. We've been spending way too damn much time here the past three days decorating for the Christmas party.

The whole place is lit up with Christmas cheer, and it feels nice. Working together has put Gemma and I a little more at peace even if we're still not besties again. There haven't been any insults flung at Pan and me either, which is a start.

We walk under the mistletoe, and Kratos and Ares both come to greet us at the entrance.

"You know, ladies," Kratos says, rubbing his hands together like a damn cartoon villain, "That's supposed to mean you kiss."

"What the fuck, Kratos? If you want a show, you're going to have to pay us for it. The problem is, you can't afford us," Gemma comments, making Ares crack up before bringing Calli in for a hug.

"You all did a great job. It's even put Zeus in a good mood."

"Isn't it more of a miracle to see you in a good mood?" Calli teases him, and he gives her a noogie as if she's his little sister. Their dynamic amuses me since Ares is known for being such an asshole and a hot head. But whenever Calli is in the room, one look, and he calms down for her.

It makes me think of Gemma and Pan a little. It's a little less out in the open, but he's definitely done a lot to protect her over the years. It's why we've just recently gotten involved in club business—he hasn't wanted Gemma around the life at all.

I catch sight of him playing pool in the corner and walk over to the tree first. It's massive. Totally Pearl and Gemma's doing. They went over the top with it. I swear, it looks like something we'd find at The Galleria or Times Square.

I place the wrapped package I have in my hands for Pan down at the bottom before going over to him. I lean against him as he waits for his turn to play pool against Poseidon.

"Gemma seems to be in a good mood today," he says.

I smile. "She would be. You know she loves Christmas."

"I do," he says. "And also," he adds, turning his head to kiss me passionately, "I'm so fucking glad you're here."

"Me too."

CHAPTER FOURTEEN

I'm not ashamed to admit the fact that the past week has been one of the best in my life. I thought that getting into the club as a member was a true high, and it was, but now, I know there are even bigger and better things out there for me.

Trix has been by my side most of the time, or me by hers. I've mostly been ignoring the fuck out of Gemma to the point of annoyance on her end while consistently coming over to see Trix. Seeing as the holidays are coming up, she's had a lot of orders in the way of cakes and cupcakes. The smell of flour is kind of making me sick at this point, and I can't imagine how she can continue to lick her fingers clean of all of the sugary confections. But it is still so damn cute to see her at her best in the kitchen, dancing, and singing while she makes these amazing elaborate concoctions. I could never do a thing like that.

Now, it's the Christmas party, and I'm anxious for her to show up. I've gotten some great shit, or at least what I think is great, for her as a gift, and I can't wait to see the look on her face when I give it to her. I don't even give a damn if she's gotten me anything, though I know she won't leave me out in the cold as far as that goes. I just wanted her to be here.

I asked her if she would come, I mentioned family, and it seemed just right. She is my family now in whatever twisted way you would call that. I haven't exactly said the three-word phrase that she may or may not be waiting to hear, but I think I've made my stance clear on us. We've fallen into a routine of being together and being exclusive without actually talking about the whole thing.

It's an amazing feeling, though, to be on the same wavelength as each other like we're supposed to be together or some shit.

I walk downstairs and take a look at the humongous Christmas tree that Gemma and Pearl put up. It left poor Calli and Trix to decorate most of the rest of the clubhouse because it took almost the entirety of the three days all the girls were here for Pearl and Gemma to get this tree up. I guess at least it's big enough for all of us to fit our presents down at the bottom. We've all been doing Secret Santa. It's a tradition.

I spot the present that I have sitting down there, the one for Ares. When I drew him, I knew I had to get something to razz on him. I just didn't know what. Trix helped me find the perfect present for him and even helped pick out the color. He may not get that big of a kick out of it, and in fact, it may be me getting kicked, but it'll be so damn worth it when everybody cracks up at him because of the look on his face.

All around the tree and up above around the top of the walls in the room are flashing blue icicle lights as well as some yellow lights. There's a mechanical Santa that turns on next to the bar every time you walk by him. He dances and sings songs. Honestly, he's gotten on my fucking nerves over the past few days, but who am I to judge what people like?

I know Christmas is a time of childlike happiness, and I'm not gonna take that away from anyone. I'm just gonna fucking steer clear from that edge of the bar until he's gone. Honestly, he kind of gives me the creeps.

I mentioned it to Trix yesterday, and she called me a big baby. She didn't really like the fact that I told her I was her big baby. Not into that kink, I guess. I laugh at the thought.

I head over to the pool table where Hermes, Poseidon, and Ares are hanging out. "Anyone wanna play a game with me?" I ask, starting to rack the balls. Poseidon steps up and grabs a stick.

"You're so on, but you're also so dead." I roll my eyes at his cheesy line of confidence. I'm pretty damn good at pool when I put my mind to it. Though, I still can't beat Hermes. He's kind of the master here.

He and Hades pretty much practice at all hours of the day and night. I think it helps them work out problems in their head or something.

Then the door opens, revealing all four girls have come for the party. Each of them is carrying at least one gift, if not more, in their hands.

I figured that Calli would have the most, and she has the biggest connection to the club, but Gemma's face is barely visible as she balances so many gift boxes it's not even funny.

She was like this as a kid, too, always way over-excited for Christmas. She would wake all of us up at like 5:30 in the morning to try to get us to go open the presents. And it had taken her til 12 to realize that Santa wasn't real because every time someone would tell her, she would just get mad.

As the memories of my sister come flooding back, I really hope that I can patch up the relationship with her at some point. She means the world to me. But the thing is, that's how much Trix means too. And my happiness is important to think about as well. I can't do everything based on Gemma's whims anymore, no matter how much I want to protect her. So, for now, I love her from afar until she's ready to really talk this through.

But at least she's smiling today. And I haven't gotten any disparaging texts either, which must be a good sign.

I lock eyes with Trix, and she blushes. I just can't get over how much of an effect I have on her. I'm used to women fawning over me for sexual attention. I have thought I was a catch, but it also makes me cocky and an asshole. I never thought I deserved much, much less would find anyone who would truly see me for everything that I am and like me.

Not just like me but possibly love me. But Trix fits the bill in so many ways. And I wouldn't have it any other way than it to be her.

Trixie's sexy, but she's also damn strong. Nobody else could handle being in my life like that.

I watch her take the one gift in her hand over to the tree and set it down before she walks over to me. I know I've got a goofy grin on my face, and Poseiden elbows me in the ribs. "I may want to cream you here, but I don't want it to be because you're too goo-goo-eyed to pay attention," Poseidon says, bringing me back to the game.

It's not my turn, but I get the feeling that my watching Trix is also distracting him. I'm kind of spaced out like that lately and wonder if this is what it's like to be in love or if this is just infatuation.

I hope it's the former because I can't imagine being without Trix. She showed me a lot about life and how much more fun life can be next to somebody else. I don't want to lose that or have to start over with somebody else. They'll never be her, anyway.

I'm waiting for my turn, and Trix comes up to lean against me.

"Gemma seems to be in a good mood today," I tell her, hoping it means they've made up. That's the worst part of this, watching the two of them be on the outs. They've been inseparable since Trix moved into the house. I hate that I'm part of the cause of their trouble.

Trix smiles. "She would be. You know she loves Christmas."

"I do," I answer. "And also," I add, turning my head to kiss her for good luck, "I'm so fucking glad you're here."

"Me too."

It's the damn truth too. I think it's going to be a great fucking day whether she ends up in my bed or not, though, of course, I hope she will.

Poseidon finally misses, and I see my chance. I could probably get two in one shot this turn.

Trixie moves away to lean against the wall, smacking my ass playfully as I bend over to try and get the perfect angle with the cue. I line it up, biting my tongue as I hit that ball, two of the stripes going into pockets.

"Yes."

"You're such a school kid, Pan," Poseidon says to me.

"You're only saying that because you're trying to save face for when I kick your ass," I say back as I shoot again and get another.

"C'mon, go easy on him," Hermes says with a laugh that causes Poseidon to give him a deadly look. It just makes Trix and I both start laughing. We MC men are totally big babies.

The game comes down to the wire, and it could be either of us winning. The club is getting crowded now, with ol' ladies, kids, family members, and girlfriends of all kinds filling the place. The mood is good, and the best part of it is there are no Vile Serpents here to ruin it.

Thorn's still out there somewhere, and we'll get him in time, but seeing as he's mostly on his own now, he wouldn't dare show his ugly face here with all of us. I don't know what he's up to, but it doesn't matter because it's fucking Christmas.

"Secret Santa time, round 'em up!" Zeus hollers. The men of the MC all gather in an oval in the center of the room past the bar while the others watch from all different places of the clubhouse. A prospect goes and begins to pull the gifts from a tree that are labeled for Secret Santa to the club members and passes them out.

Hermes is next to me, and he begins to rattle his like he's gonna figure out what's in there.

"Better hope whatever the fuck that is, isn't breakable." He thinks about it and then stops instantly. "Great job you're doing there," I joke, slapping his back.

"Shut the fuck up," he says.

Zeus drawls on with a speech about working together for the good of the whole and Christmas time.

I'm mostly tuning the whole thing out since I know there are other presents waiting over there for us to hand over to each other, especially from the girls. Those are a little much more special than this silly Secret Santa, although I do appreciate it.

I have one box set in front of me, and I wonder who it's from. It's small in a powder blue color with a black ribbon around it. It's tied meticulously, so it had to be someone who pays attention to detail. I'm not sure, but I'll find out soon enough.

All the guys started opening their shit, and some of the gifts were excellent, some were downright shitty, and others were clearly meant to jab at the receiver.

We're having a good ol' time, and then Ares goes to open his. On the inside will be a little card to let him know it's from me. But he's gonna flip the fuck out when he sees what it is.

He rips into it like a kid at the candy store getting a Wonka Bar and then stares down at the contraption almost in confusion until it dawns on him. By this point, we're already laughing at him.

In his hand is a big, sparkly, pink dildo. Between the titters, I tell him, "I figured if you're going to act like something's up your ass, then something should actually be up it," before cracking up again. Poseidon is full-on snorting, and Zeus is slapping his knee. Apparently, it was the best gag gift ever, though I know I'm gonna get shit from Ares for it later. So worth it.

I go to open mine and find out it's actually from Zeus. It's a chain and on the end of that chain is a little vial of what looks like glitter. "Fairy dust for Pan," Zeus says with a shrug.

I'm not too proud to wear such a thing, so I immediately fasten it behind my neck. "Perfect. Just what I wanted," I say, and everyone begins to laugh again.

Once Secret Santa is all wrapped up, I pull Trix to the side. "Come on, let's open our presents." I go and grab not just the gifts I have for her but also the gift box that she placed at the bottom of the tree when she came in, knowing it's mine. In fact, it has my name on it.

I lead her to the top of the stairs, and that's where we sit. She sits herself down next to me on the step above me.

"Go on. I want you to open yours first." I nod toward her presents, and she starts looking over all three packages trying to figure out what she should open first. "Now I feel kind of bad. I only got you the one thing, and you got me three?"

I wave my arm at her, letting her know it's not a big deal. "I'm fine with whatever you got me, even if it's nothing. Before you go feeling all bad about it, you probably spent way more than I did on one item than I did on several. Just open them."

She smiles at my enthusiasm and begins ripping into the first one. The look on her face when she pulls out the half-human skull that's meant to be a phone holder tells me everything I need to know about whether I did a good job or not.

I've noticed at her house before how she really likes kind of bohemian gothic decor, so I figured the skull would be a good touch. "For your bedside table," I tell her, and she hugs me around the neck. "Wow, that's really good for this one. Wait for the others," I tell her.

Moving on to the next one, Trix pulls out a red necklace. Not just any red necklace, but the chain is silver, and it dangles down to between her breasts. It's in the shape of the tree of life with a crystal in the center. She puts it on immediately. "It's gorgeous," she tells me.

"It isn't over yet," I tell her, pointing to the third package. She takes her time on this one, getting piece by piece of wrapping paper off. Inside, she finds a pack of white candles with runes carved into them. "Took me forever to find these, I knew I had to get something that was just right for you, and I felt like this was it. If you don't like them, we can return them."

She looks up at me and then down at the candles longingly. "I'll definitely be utilizing one of those tonight."

"I'm so glad you liked them all. I was so afraid I was doing the wrong thing when I was picking them out."

"No, not at all. I just hope that the one present I was able to get you is as good, in your eyes, as these are in mine."

I'm so curious to see what it is now to prove to her it's perfect. I open my present, wondering why the damn package is so big, and then I see it.

She's gotten me what I know is an expensive as fuck custom helmet for when I'm on my bike. Not many take bike safety seriously around here, but I'm more likely to now, considering she's made it look like it's something Batman would wear if he really drove a Harley.

"Holy fuck, this is probably the best and most personal present anyone's gotten me other than my own mother."

She scoffs at the usage of my mother, which would normally make me laugh too, but all I want to do is try it out.

"Really, though," I say, "it's the truth. No one ever thinks of me like that."

"Well, now someone does."

CHAPTER FIFTEEN

I roll the candles between my fingers to get a feel for them. I can't believe he didn't only get me candles, but he got candles with runes carved in them, not even knowing what it would mean to me. "So, you really like those, huh?" Pan asks, watching me.

I smile up at him, pulling myself out of my trance. "Yes, possibly the best present anyone's ever given to me. It's crazy how you know me so well in such a short period of time."

He smirks. "You probably give me a little bit too much credit considering I can find a million things just like this all over your room. I've even seen a bunch at the house, and I know they don't belong to Gemma, and they were there long before Calli showed up. That only leaves you or Pearl being responsible for them, and I just don't see Pearl as the type to have these kinds of things."

I laugh a little. "No, she's really not. She loves books, though. I really hope that the one I got her she doesn't have yet. It's kind of hard to shop for her because of it. I swear she's read every damn book in every library in the United States." We both laugh at that, and I grab my stomach. I've been doing a lot of that tonight, and my muscles hurt from it. It's that good kind of hurt when you've had a great night filled with joy.

"So, what is it you do with them anyway?" Pan asks, picking one up and looking at it. "I have no idea what any of this means."

I place a hand on his shoulder. "Don't worry, I'm happy to teach you. But I'm kind of glad you asked because after the shit with your arm last week, it's left me a little scared. Would you mind if I did like a protection candle for you in your room? That way, I can also show you how it works."

"A candle can protect me?" He raises his eyebrows skeptically. I grab his hand and yank him up the stairs toward his room. I'm just going to have to show him what I mean.

"I'm going to need something that I can stand the candle up on. It could even be a glass at this point if you don't have anything else," I tell him, clearing off some room on his nightstand. He goes away and comes back with a shot glass. "That'll work," I tell him sitting down on his bed and facing the nightstand.

He passes me the glass, and I put the correct candle in it. "Lighter, please," I tell him.

He hands it to me but then holds my wrist. I look up at him, and he's biting his lip. It's so sexy, and I'm temporarily distracted, but I'm not sure we need to rehash having sex for everyone to hear again, considering Gemma is right downstairs along with everyone, including children, this time. Maybe not the best way to make a good impression on everyone for Christmas.

"A little bossy tonight, aren't we?" he asks, licking his lips.

I roll my eyes, but I'm smiling. "Just give me the damn lighter," I tell him. He lets go of my wrist and watches me.

"You see this symbol here?" I ask him, pointing to the rune on the candle I'm about to light. He nods his head. "It's called a rune. Lots of different cultures had runes, but these happen to be Celtic in nature. This one represents protection. So, candles and anything else that contains a lot of energy or uses one of the elements, you can kind of bend to your will. I know it sounds weird but keep an open mind."

He watches me intently without judgment as I light the candle. The flame sparks, and I close my eyes, my hand hovering above the flame and feeling the warmth. I make a slight humming noise as I set my intent for the candle. I will it to wrap a protection around him. That way, the next time he has to face the Serpents, hopefully, he'll still only maintain a laceration from a stray bullet or less.

I open my eyes and smile. "So, you see, heat and fire have energy. I mean, that part is basic science, really. I'm just shaping the energy into something I want it to be. In this case, I've asked the candle to protect you from harm. So no more getting grazed by bullets, right?" I ask him while looking up at him.

"I'll damn well try my best. Like I said, I'm not going anywhere anytime soon." He pulls me from my sitting position and into his arms, giving me a kiss that makes me go weak at the knees. He's really trying to tempt me here.

"Why don't we go back downstairs and see if the girls want to exchange gifts. I think a couple of them even have stuff for Zeus. Then, maybe we should get out of here or something."

He wiggles his eyebrows at me, and I laugh while slapping him playfully on the chest. I would say everything is innuendo with him, but I kind of mean the same thing.

I don't think I'm going to be able to keep my hands off of him forever tonight. Plus, it's a perfect excuse to make use of my gifts. I can burn a cleansing candle and a protection candle for the house when we get there, and I can go ahead and set up my phone holder on my bedside table.

I walk around him and head for the stairs again, taking them quickly so he can't snatch me up and pull me back upstairs. But I feel his longing stare behind me all the way down.

I find Calli with Eros with her father already. "Hey guys, why don't we open our gifts for each other?" I suggest.

"You two in a hurry or something?" Zeus teases, and something about him saying it makes me turn bright red. He cracks up at me, his raspy laugh then setting off Pan as well.

"Maybe a little," I admit

Calli volunteers to go grab Pearl and Gemma since I have no idea how Gemma would react if I asked her to come exchange gifts with me. I don't even know if she got me a gift or not. It's irrelevant. I got her one, though.

We all go stand by the tree, and Calli bends over and begins to pull up the presents that are for us, sitting them down at our feet. There's nowhere to sit down since there are so many people, and every space to lounge or sit is taken up by others, but I love the warm atmosphere it creates. It's probably the most unique Christmas celebration I've ever been to.

Everyone chooses Zeus to go first, and he has a couple of presents. One from Calli and one from Gemma. I examine the one from Gemma and just know it's probably going to be a gag gift or something. He picks up the gift from Calli first and goes to shake it, but she stops him. "Don't do that. What if you break it?" she cries out.

"Well, I guess that tells me something about it," Zeus says, giving her a wink. Calli rolls her eyes and gestures for him to go ahead and just open it. When he does, he finds an entire beard care kit as well as a comb set and some fancy cologne.

Zeus leans over and gives Calli a hug. "It sure is nice having you around now."

"Thanks, Dad. I feel the same way. Thanks for making it feel like home to me."

"Okay, okay, no need to tear up," Zeus says, picking up Gemma's gift and trying to hide any emotion he has. "This one doesn't sound breakable, Gemma," he says.

"Come on, Zeus, just open the damn thing," Gemma says, putting her hands on her hips. We all laugh, and Zeus rips it open. I can see the look of horror in Calli's eyes as we all realize what's in it. I would bet right about now she wants to burn her eyes out. Because not only is there a pack of boxers inside, but there is a bright red man-thong that he pulls out and admires. He begins putting it up to his hips as if he's imagining what it's going to look like.

I cover my mouth as I begin to laugh. I'm trying to hold it in as Calli turns around and practically retches. "What the hell, Gemma," Calli says, not even looking at her father anymore. "Did you really have to do that to me?"

Zeus just smirks. "See, I knew you had a crush on me, Gemma."

"No! Nope! Absolutely not!" Calli says, throwing her hands up in the air. "This is not okay at all. Dad, stop it."

Pan doubles over at that point, grabbing his stomach. If I don't let it go, I'm probably going to pee myself trying to hold my laughter in, so I just start to cackle.

It's so like Gemma to get him a gift like this. Trolling both Zeus and Calli at the same time. She just adds fuel to the fire when she says, "What better gift than to let the old man know he still got it?"

"Then I guess that's so very damn thoughtful of you, Gemma, but did you have to do it by giving him a banana hammock in front of his daughter? Was that really necessary?"

Gemma ignores Calli and begins to scratch her chin as if she's thinking, looking Zeus up and down. "I hope I got you the right size. I've been looking at your shoes for a couple weeks to try and determine." At that point, Calli straight up walks away and goes to the bathroom. She's probably throwing up, and I turn to Pan and laugh into his chest.

"Well, I'm not sure any of the gifts can top that one," Pearl comments. "But I think I'll keep us moving along." Pearl opens her gifts from everyone, all books or gift cards to get books, of course. She's probably the happiest one among us, though, and doesn't care at all that one of the books she got is something she already has because it's a different book cover.

By the time Gemma is opening her presents, Calli is back. No one dares mention the underwear again, and Zeus has tucked them back into the box and put them to the side, thank goodness.

Gemma is a little bit more complicated to shop for. She likes experiences more than she likes things, but I actually bought her the gift before we had our falling out over me fucking her brother. It's a pair of tickets to a concert for her favorite band. We've actually seen them live once before when we first became friends. I thought she might want to go with me, but I suppose now she'll probably go with someone else. Which is totally fine, as long as she's happy.

When she opens them, she looks at me and says the first few words she's said in days, which is just a simple, "Thank you." I guess if she's not yelling at me or insulting Pan or me, it's an improvement.

Once I open mine, I end up with another necklace and a lot more candles. There's no gift from Gemma, but I'm not exactly surprised. I'm sure once we makeup, she'll get me something then. Pan and I say our goodbyes, and then we're out, and I'm hopping on his bike.

I watch his excitement as he puts on his new custom helmet. He loves the damn thing. It's pretty cute, actually. I wrap my arms around him, and we ride off. "Hey, can we stop for food or something? I know not a lot's open, but I'm pretty hungry," I ask as we hit a red light.

"How about some sushi?" he asks.

"Where the hell are we gonna get sushi on Christmas?"

"No worries, I've got this." Pan turns off on a different road and then pulls up to a gas station. Obviously, it's one of the only things open. It's kind of odd being here with most of the lights off in the neighborhood. All the other businesses are shut down for the holiday, and even most of the houses have their lights off by this time of night other than the Christmas lights that still hang on the outside of the houses.

We go inside and pick out our sushi, though I'm not sure how I feel about eating it from a gas station. I swear I've heard so many horror stories about that, but I just go with the flow. It's a good night, so why ruin it by complaining?

We grab some chopstix as well and then head out to the lot to eat it. I lean up against the bike while he leans up against the wall on the side of the building, where the light shines down on him.

I point my chopstix at him as I open up my sushi. "This better not get me sick, Pan," I tell him with a grin.

"Look, it may not be top-notch, but it hasn't caused me any trouble yet," he says, his hand up in a sign of surrender.

"You don't know that it isn't because you have an iron stomach," I say, taking my first bite tentatively. He simply laughs at me.

My salmon roll is actually pretty damn good for the fact it was less than $10 and from a corner gas station, not even a major chain. And it's been a while since I've had any sushi at all.

We savor the moment together, talking a few times about the presents we got and how we plan to enjoy the fuck out of them, and we eventually get back on the bike.

I'm getting used to the feel of being on the back of it and can kind of see why there's a thrill associated with it. Not just a thrill but just a general feeling of being alive and in the moment. Being so close to everything surrounding us, rather than inside a car, connects us more to what's around us and causes us to pay closer attention. Not to mention the contact with Pan can be intoxicating. There isn't a barrier to us being together this way.

Maybe it's the spiritualist in me talking, but there's something special about all of it.

When we get home, there's still no one else around. I pull my key out of my purse and let us both inside.

"You think Calli's going to be staying with Eros tonight?" Pan asks as I shut and lock the door behind us, and he flips on the light in the living room. I look at him with hooded eyes, knowing what he's asking. But I know I want to light my candles first. Plus, they can set a good ambiance for us.

"Probably, but Pearl and Gemma will be home eventually," I tell him, though I don't know if I actually care. "Feel free to turn on the TV or relax. I am going to make use of a couple of my new candles." I beam at him, and he laughs at me before hopping onto the couch and kicking off his shoes. I make a mental note of the scene. I kind of like the way he looks there.

I pull out my candles and go over to the small bookshelf we have sitting in the entryway. All my supplies are already there. I use it as an altar of sorts, though I have a more detailed one in the bedroom. This one is simply what I use to help the whole house versus myself, and I was so relieved when Gemma didn't make a big deal about it when I moved in. Some people can get weirded out about all the spiritual stuff.

I place one candle on each side of the shelf inside the holders I have for them. One for cleansing and one for protection, and then I light them. I turn the lights off as I see that Pan is browsing Netflix for a movie.

"Ooh, are we going to watch a Christmas movie?" I ask him, sitting down next to him and relaxing.

"Yeah, you can't have Christmas without a Christmas movie." He surprises me by putting it on White Christmas, and I scoot close to him, his arm around me. It's so normal I could cry. How the hell did I end up here, with a guy I really care about, on my couch and watching a Christmas movie without a care in the world?

I find myself singing some of the songs as the movie goes along, and Pan joins in with me. His hands are all over me for a lot of it, and I feel like I could scream for release at this point, but I'm also really enjoying spending time with him this way. It's nearly perfect.

Pearl and Gemma still haven't come home, and I wonder if Gemma is fucking one of the MC guys again or maybe just gonna stay and hang out with Calli. Pearl's probably found a cozy corner to curl up in and start reading one of her books. I smile at the image it conjures.

Pan's hand is sliding up my thigh and squeezing, but then he pulls me up onto his lap. I squirm and complain about not being able to see the movie, but there's no real fight in me. I'm exactly where I want to be.

"You're the most beautiful woman in the world," he says to me out of the blue, and something about how he looks at me and the way he says it makes me feel settled and calm inside. Even though I'm pretty damn good at being strong and collected, especially on the outside, I never feel much other than turmoil on the inside unless I'm meditating with my crystals and candles. The fact that a person can make me this content blows my mind.

I lean in and kiss him, the one time I'm actually dressed up in a skirt being great timing as my panties grind up against the bulge in his jeans. I think about the term making love and wonder if I've ever felt it before other than him. No, I don't think I have. I hope this lasts. Secretly, I hope it lasts forever.

I begin to rub against him more vigorously, my panties soaked with my need for him as he kisses me, enjoying the way he drives me insane. His hands snake up and down my back, doing those soothing, light touches he does. How can he make me feel so relaxed and keyed up at the same time?

Without a care in the world, I reach between us to unbutton his jeans and unzip them, tugging him out of them before continuing to slide up against him. The movement moves my panties to the side, the lace no match for our want of each other.

He slides in with ease as I glide over him, and he grabs my ass under my skirt as I raise up and glide back down again, pumping him in and out of me with shaky breaths.

"Oh god," the moan pours out of me as the sensation hits me like a ton of bricks. My nerves are sending little lightning bolts back and forth, and I sink into the feeling.

I unbutton my top as he squeezes my ass cheeks and hips, moving me over him as he meets me thrust for thrust. My nipples are hard from being so aroused, and Pan leans forward to flick his tongue across the sensitive flesh there. "Mmmm," I say as he continues, making them super sensitive and reactive. He wraps his mouth around my left breast and begins to suck. I lean into the sensation and pick up my pace.

"Oh, fuck," I say unabashedly.

The door opens, and the light flicks on unexpectedly. I pull my shirt closed as Pan pulls back, and Pearl screams. Pan screams, and I follow suit before all of us start laughing. My face grows hot as I realize Pan and I have been caught in the act.

Unsure what else to do, I stay on top of him to keep him covered up, and it's awkward as fuck. "Hurry up and get to your room," I tell Pearl.

She purses her lips at me, but I can tell she's not mad, just shocked. "That's where y'all should be instead of the couch," she lectures but goes to her room anyway, closing the door a little more loudly than usual.

I bury my face in Pan's chest and giggle for a moment, catching my breath before I get off of him. I stand up and offer my hand. "C'mon, Gemma is still not home. We'll go to my room," I tell him.

He takes my hand, and I practically drag him into the bedroom, where he pushes me down on the end of the bed and pulls my ass to the edge. He tugs my panties off me and places a leg on either side of his neck.

He leaves me exposed with a grin on his face while he slides his pants and boxers down, his cock dripping with a mixture of precum and me before he slides himself back in. I arch my neck back and moan, wondering how us being in here helps, considering Pearl can definitely hear us. Hopefully, she'll put some headphones on or something because I don't think there's any holding back tonight.

I slide my legs down his body to around his hips and then squeeze, tugging him toward me. He goes deeper, and my eyes roll into the back of my head with pleasure.

"You like me filling you up, don't you?" he asks me in a gruff voice as he slows his thrusts down to a painful pace. I just want him to consume me at this point. I want to lose all control of my body as I am wracked with shivers of ecstasy.

"Yes," I moan back to him, a little whimper in my voice. "More, please."

"Oh, so now my baby's begging. Okay." He slams into me, and I shut my eyes and bite my lip. He does it again and again until he can't handle it anymore, either.

He screams my name as he climaxes, and I cum soon after.

CHAPTER SIXTEEN

PAN

My phone buzzes, and I get up out of habit, waking up to the sound. I slide over, trying not to wake Trix up as I grab it. I see instantly that it's a notification from Zeus. I stand up and tuck my jeans on as quietly and quickly as I can before sliding out of Trixie's room. I go into the living room and turn on a lamp, pulling up the text message on my phone.

The display clock tells me that it's just after two in the morning.

I start reading the thread, and I realize it's a group message. Zeus and Hades are discussing that there is a strange car sitting right outside of our territory. It's actually sitting in one of the lots that we own.

What's even stranger is that this lot has no trespassing signs up everywhere. There's no mistaking it, and most everyone knows that it's MC territory. So it's super suspicious that anyone would be out there, especially at this time of night.

I need to send a team out to look at it. If you're available, please let me know.

I answer Zeus' message and know that while I'd rather be here with Trix, she's asleep, and it's best to be there to support the club. Plus, while at least one officer should come out with us, it's best to save the officers for when it's something more serious. Reconnaissance missions don't require that. So, I go ahead and volunteer. It's not like it's going to take me all night.

I'm in. I'm just over at Gemma's place.

Zeus ends up sending out a team of Dion, myself, Ares, and Thanatos. I guess at least we'll have Ares on our side if some shit goes down. He's enough to scare the living hell out of anybody, honestly.

I follow the directions from the lot in question to the meet-up spot on the other side of the block. We all cut our engines and park in a gas station's lot before heading over. When we get over to the lot, it's pitch black.

Not only is it 2:30 in the morning, but there's only one lamp on the entire lot. It's by the building that sits on the plot of land here, and there it is, a car just chilling. If I were to come across it randomly, I would assume it was just either someone doing a drug deal or someone thinking that it's an abandoned parking lot where they're not going to get caught fucking each other, but the fact that it's been here a while and it's specifically our territory with everything that's been going on with the Serpents, better safe than sorry.

"I don't know what it is because I can't place from where, but I recognize that car," Thanatos says. I get chills when he says it. We begin to approach, at this point, making ourselves known. The tension is palpable, all of us ready to grab our guns at a moment's notice because we don't know how this asshole is going to react. Especially if whoever it is knows who we are. But then the car just speeds off.

"Damn it," Ares says. Dion tries to calm him down, but Ares begins to shake the fence around the lot in anger.

"Come on, we need to go back to the clubhouse and let Zeus know what went down," Thanatos says. "He'll want to know, and you don't wanna make a scene at this time of night."

Ares growled like a wild animal but followed us all to our bikes anyway. Instead of getting right back to Trix, I have to ride back to the clubhouse. When I get there and park, I pull up my phone real quick to text her. I don't want her thinking I just left her there for no reason.

Hey, I didn't want to leave you, but there was important club business. Hopefully, I'll see you tomorrow.

We all go inside and find Zeus in his office, but he's half asleep and drunk off his ass. A bottle of rum sits on his desk, nearly drained. "I'll shoot a text to Hades to let him know we're back, and we don't know who it is. We'll meet first thing in the morning," Ares says, having cooled down some.

We all trudge up the stairs to our rooms, and I'm honestly exhausted. I had been in such a good rhythm of sleep laying there right next to Trixie before I got interrupted by the text, and now I just need to crash.

I lay down and fall almost instantly to sleep. Still in the same clothes I had on at the party. They smell like her, and at least that's a comfort.

When I wake up to my alarm the next morning screaming at me that I need to put some laundry on and then meet with the others to go over what the fuck happened with that car, I check my text messages to see if I've heard back from Trix.

I instantly feel guilty.

Trix: It's okay. I woke up at 4 a.m. Sushi made me SO sick. I feel like shit.

Me: Fuck. Sorry, babe. That's my fault.

Trix: No, I had fun anyway.

Me:Still, I'll have to plan to take you on a proper date soon. One with fresh-made sushi.

She sends back a crying laughing emoji, and at least I don't have to worry so much about her. I guess I do have an iron stomach, though, because I feel alright. Maybe it's just all the blood and shit I've seen. I just don't feel anything in my gut anymore.

I shake my head and then strip my bed down and grab the pile of clothes I have in the corner of the room, heading over to the laundry room. I pass Calli on the way, bringing what looks like some coffee back to Eros' room.

"You're up early," she mentions. "I made some fresh coffee if you need it."

"Thanks. I probably will. There was a thing with the club last night. I got called away from Trix for it. I have to meet with Hades and Zeus in a bit."

"Good luck with that. My dad is going to be pretty hungover. He drank enough for a whale."

I chuckle. "Wouldn't be the first time, thanks." I go to walk away with my bundle of laundry when I remember something. "Hey, is Gemma around? Did she ever make it home? I left Trix at 2 a.m., and her truck still wasn't there."

I don't like the uncomfortable look on Calli's face when she scrambles for an answer. "Pretty sure she's still here," she says, not giving anything else away.

"Thanks." I don't expect her to break girl code for me as long as Gemma's safe, but it's something I can talk to her about later down the road. Because if she's still here, she's staying with someone. Now, she could just be with one of the few female club members or one of the clubwhores. But I know the alternative is more likely, and I don't want to think about that right now. First, I know she could be doing it to get back at me for being with Trix, and I don't want that kind of drama the day after Christmas.

I shelf the issue and put my laundry on before heading downstairs to find Thanatos and Dion at the bar. "Prez is just getting some coffee," Dion informs me.

"I bet he is. I think I'll grab some too."

I run into Zeus on the way to the kitchen, and he nearly spills his overflowing cup of inky black shit. He always likes his coffee strong and plain, but I guess with him trying to sober up, it makes sense.

I grab my own cup, a splash of milk and a lot of sugar going into it and meet up with the guys over at the bar, who have now been joined by a very grumpy-looking Ares.

I want to make a comment about how he's missing his beauty sleep, but I know I'll get my nose broken if I do right now. So, instead, I break the ice and start talking about what happened the night before.

Before long, Hades comes up to us to join in the conversation, catching up on the description of the car and that it drove off the moment whoever the driver was saw us.

"That's just fuckin' weird," Hades says.

"Yeah, I don't like that shit. We're gonna have to see if the security cameras were working and caught the plates or something. Find out any other details we can and get the plates run."

"I'm on it," Thanatos volunteers.

"Great, let me know what you find out and make sure you give Hermes the details."

"Sure thing, Prez."

Even though we have a plan of action, an uneasy feeling hits the pit of my stomach. Thorn out in the world causing shit and chaos, missing a weird car in our territory, losing business from the street drugs. I think it all adds up to something fishy, but I don't understand the math well enough to add it all up.

CHAPTER SEVENTEEN

Y'all need to come to Shots. We're going to celebrate

It's the day before New Year's Eve, and I wake up from a nap to that text message from Pan. Apparently, he sent it out to all of us. The whole club is supposed to be going to *Shots* for an early new year celebration since it's New Year's Eve. All of the bars and clubs will be too packed. I've been napping on and off for the last few days because my body is just not wanting to recover from this food poisoning I got.

I've already made a vow to myself to never eat gas station sushi again. That shit is rank, apparently, and my stomach cannot handle it. I'm better than I was, and I don't plan on missing out on seeing Pan and getting to celebrate with everyone. I just am probably not going to be drinking much, considering my stomach is still turning.

I can barely keep anything down, and it's becoming more than a minor inconvenience, considering the fact that I actually have to bake cakes and cupcakes for various parties for a living. I gag every time I have to taste the icing or the batter.

That gas station food was a horrible idea, but I don't blame Pan for it. He was just trying to make it a fun date night even though nothing was open.

I go casual, pulling on some ripped-up jeans and a black crop top with a skull on the front of it. I put a matching beanie on my head and don't even bother running the brush through my hair. I swipe some eyeliner under my eyes and call it good. And I stick to just flat boots considering heels would have me wobbling all around with the fact that I haven't really eaten much over the past several days. Nothing I've kept down, anyway.

I come out of my room to find Calli pulling her jacket on. "So, you are gonna come with us?" she asks with a smile. She came into my room earlier to say that she hoped I'd be able to go even though I didn't feel good because she was hoping that this would be another chance for Gemma and me to make up. Even though Christmas went well, she went back to giving me the cold shoulder afterward.

"Yeah, I figure maybe I'll have a drink, something mild, and otherwise, I'll stick to some ginger ale. I'm still not my 100% self, but I'm a lot better than I was. I think this is finally passing."

Calli gives me a hug, and then the honk of the horn on a bike interrupts us. "That will be my ride," she says, walking toward the door in her stilettos. I don't know how she does that shit. She goes outside and gets on the back of Eros's bike, and I watch as they ride off together.

Can you come pick me up? I don't know about riding with Gemma.

I shoot the text over to Pan, and he texts me back immediately.

You two still aren't talking? Also, I'm already on my way.

I shouldn't be surprised. Of course, he's on his way. Any chance to get me on the back of that motorcycle with him. He tells me how he loves the feel of me wrapping my arms around him while he's riding.

Maybe the fresh air will do me some good.

Gemma and Pearl come out of their rooms, both already dressed and ready to go. Gemma breezes right past me, flipping her red hair behind her head. Pearl gives me an apologetic look and fixes her flannel shirt. "See you there?" she asks me, and I nod.

"Yep, for a little bit. Just waiting on my ride." Pearl gives the thumbs up and then follows Gemma out the door. I hear the engine turning over in the big blue truck, letting me know that they're about to go. Just as they pull out, I catch the distinct sound of the engine of a motorcycle pulling into the parking lot. I grab my bag and rush out without thinking, clenching my stomach as I realize that this may be a bad idea.

I carefully climb onto the back of the bike while Pan is grinning from ear to ear. "Glad to see you up at about, but can you handle the ride?"

"Yeah, I'll be fine. I may need to go home early, though. If I need to get a ride with somebody else, that's okay. I don't want to ruin your night."

"If you're with me, how could it ruin my night?" he asks me cheesily. I roll my eyes and motion for him to get going.

When we pull up to *Shots*, the cool breeze has given me a little bit of red on my cheeks, but it feels better on my throat and stomach. Being outside has calmed me. There are already bikes lined up in the parking lot two by two. Seems like *Shots* is gonna be full of Sons of Gods tonight and not much else.

Inside, there are a few people sitting around from other clubs. But it looks like it's pretty much all bikers other than me, Pearl, Gemma, and Calli. Pan pulls me out a seat at the table, and I sit between Calli and Pearl. Gemma, Eros, and Pan are on the other side of the table. Zeus is a couple of tables behind us, giving some kind of half-drunk toast, letting me know he's already been partying for a while.

Everything seems to be in place, and I settle into my seat.

The waiter comes over, and I quickly order a ginger ale, my stomach starting to turn again. Some of the people around me already have food, and for some reason, it just all smells like shit. This is definitely not the kind of diet I want to be on.

It gets worse as I wait for my ginger ale to come, and I have no choice but to run to the bathroom. I've only been here like what five, maybe ten minutes? I clutch my bag and get up from the chair, glad that I have those to-go toothbrushes in my bag just in case. I'm going to need them after I puke my guts out in the *Shots* bathroom.

Pan shoots me a worried look, but I ignore it and try my best just to get to the bathroom on time. When I get inside, luckily, I'm the only person in there. I throw one of the stall doors open, barely making it as my knees fall to the floor. I hang my head over the bowl, frantically tugging my hair up and out of the way as I puke my guts out over and over.

My bag lays limply next to me, holding my only safety nets: nausea medicine, Pepto Bismol, and my travel toothbrushes.

I wait until I feel I'm done retching before slowly standing up. I'm a little dizzy, and I'm sure it's because I haven't had much to eat. I'm probably going to have to order something, even if it's just a piece of toast or some cheese or something. Maybe even plain chicken, if I'm lucky. I make my way over to the sink, clutching my bag. I pull out my toothbrush and turn on the warm water. I take some deep breaths in time with the running water before I wet my toothbrush and begin to scrub. I spit several times, making sure I get all of that acid taste and smell out.

I so badly want to be here with everyone and try and make things up with Gemma, but I don't know how much more I'm going to be able to handle. I pray that maybe it's just the ride over and getting used to all the smells of food. Maybe it'll pass now that I've thrown up, and I'll have some ginger ale and be fine.

I put everything away back in my purse, my mind preoccupied as I walk out of the bathroom. Somehow, I don't notice anyone there and end up walking straight into somebody. I can tell by the fact that I basically hit a wall of muscle that it's a guy.

"I'm so sorry. I guess I wasn't paying enough attention." I go to walk around, but then I meet his eyes, and my body freezes. My eyes roam his face, and I know I haven't escaped him this time.

It's him, the priest from Iowa, the one who stars in my nightmares pretty damn frequently now. He's standing in front of me in an MC cut of all things and smiling down at me. Other than looking a little older now and a little worse for the wear with some sunspots, he doesn't look any less strong or intimidating. In fact, he probably looks even worse, considering he's in an MC.

I notice his patch on his cut, and it says, chaplain. That means he's leading his club in faith. I just want to turn around back into the bathroom and vomit, but I know I'm trapped. I don't know if he recognizes me or not, but I want to get away from him now. I need to find a way to make sure he lets me go. Then I can go wait outside or in the car while this all goes down. Maybe then the memories insisting on coming through the forefront of my mind might subside.

But the thought of what he might be using his position for starts running through my mind over and over as I try to think what to say.

"That's okay. Kind of glad you ran into me, actually," he says, snaking his arms up the sides of the walls, nonchalantly blocking me in. He's big enough that I probably couldn't even squeeze under them and in between his side and the wall if I needed to.

"I'm here with someone," I say shyly with a smile, tucking my hair behind my ear. Maybe he's just flirting with me in general, and this will get him to leave me alone. But it doesn't. "Oh, come on, I just wanna catch up. You've grown up into a nice, pretty lady, I see. Not sure what I expected, but it wasn't this. I wonder if you're just as naughty as you were back then."

He cocks his head to the side like he's studying a science experiment, and I put my hand up on my mouth to try not to gag. So, he does recognize me. This is my worst nightmare come true. I just might puke all over him. He would deserve it, but I don't know if that's going to make him angry and then he's gonna lash out at me, and I don't know if anyone will get to me in time.

Thinking about when the whole MC was here, and then Calli got taken right before our eyes and dragged away, I don't know if even screaming would get someone over to me in time before he picked me up and ran. "Maybe you could back up into that bathroom there. Maybe we can rehash the past a little just for old time's sake," he says, trying to make bedroom eyes at me.

It's official. He's given me the flu. My feet feel like they're cemented into the ground, though, and I don't know what to do. Some people tense up when they face situations like this, getting ready to fight. Some people get ready to run away. But for a select few unlucky ones, we freeze. Our body is unsafe and freezing seems like the best option because if we fight, we know it's going to just be worse.

"No thanks. Like I said, I'm here with someone." My voice is shaky, too shaky. He's looking at me, thinking I'm lying even though it's true. I don't have anywhere to go but backward, and he grabs my arm, trying to force me into the bathroom. I cling to the edges of the door and try not to let him push me in. Then, something in me just snaps. I stop holding on so tightly, and I draw my hand back and then smack him across the face.

"Get the hell away from me!" I must say it louder than I realize, as the entire bar suddenly goes quiet. The noise is loud enough to get Pan's attention, and he uses his strength to force his way through the man's arm to stand between him and me.

"What the hell is this?" Pan asks, looking back and forth between us as if he were solving a school playground incident. With no answers other than my wild, deer in headlights look, he gets angry. He looks back at my living nightmare and asks, "Why do you have your hands on my ol' lady?" His tone would be enough to scare me to stop, but this isn't me. This is a monster.

Pan being there breaks the connection between his arm and mine, and Pan looks at me, his eyes wild. He's questioning what the hell this is, and I don't even know how to answer him right now. I'm sure my face is pale and filled with fear. Even though he's here, I still don't quite feel safe.

Pan turns back to the chaplain. I now notice his MC name on the patch for the first time, Smoke, as he begins to snicker in Pan's face.

"Your ol' lady and me, we're old friends," Smoke has the audacity to say. "I didn't know she was spoken for, or I wouldn't have touched her." Of course, that's udder bullshit, considering I told him I was here with someone.

Men like him only know how to tell lies anymore. Ares and Hades must notice things still aren't calming down because they come over to back Pan up. They know something's wrong with this scenario.

I feel dizzy and closed in. The only want I have right now is to get away. If I could fly to the other edge of the world, I would. Just to get away from him and this feeling in my stomach.

Ares towers over the guy and gives the back of his head a death glare. He turns around to see the two new additions, and I'm starting to worry a fight's going to break out. "Why don't you come with me, sweetheart?" Hades asks me but looks in Smoke's eyes the whole time. He reaches his hand around the guy for me to take it. Pan moves slightly out of the way so that I can, and I squeeze myself in the space between all of them so that Hades can take me away.

I almost puke, walking past Smoke, feeling his aura surrounding me. Its sickly green and black tendrils reach out to try and pull me into his realm of misery again. I can't let that happen. I can't be that girl again.

I feel horrible for causing any trouble for the bar or for the MC. I know what happened the last time someone got in a fight with somebody from another MC over the way he was treating a woman. Now a bunch of blood is on their hands, and Zeus almost died. Calli could have died too. I don't want to be the reason for something like that, but I do need to walk away. I can't be here a second longer.

I hold my breath and let Hades take me back to where everyone else is. My whole body is shaking, and I'm scared for myself if Smoke's allowed to walk out of this bar. I'm also afraid for Pan if he tries to make sure that Smoke doesn't make it out.

Gemma gets up suddenly and comes up to me before I can make it to a seat. "What the hell is that about?" She points over to the bathroom, where there's still a standoff between Pan, Ares, and Smoke.

Gemma doesn't know a whole lot about my past. She knows I was an orphan and that I was abused in an orphanage. She doesn't know the gory details, but I'm not going to lie to her either, especially with him standing right there. Everyone deserves to know what kind of shitty person he is.

Before I can psych myself out of it, I look Gemma straight in the eye and tell her. I tell her about the way that he started grooming a lot of us girls when we were young, about the way he talked about female temptation. I told her how he gave some other priests access to us but that he was the worst. How he always blamed the way we looked, the way we walked, the way we dressed for his temptations, for his sins. And how we would be punished for it.

Something about just letting it all out at once feels cathartic. I'm telling my truth, and I know Gemma is not the only one who can hear me. But maybe I'm finally safe now. These people are good people, even if they do some not good things.

Because I'm a part of the fold now, they'll protect me. And as much as I don't want to be responsible for anything bad happening to them, I need protecting right now.

"What the fuck," Gemma says under her breath before going around me and literally marching over to the bar. I watch her, confused and stunned, as she goes behind the bar to grab the baseball bat that Calli has had to use on a couple of occasions, thanks to rowdy MC members.

What the hell is she doing?

It doesn't compute until it's too late to stop her. She walks over to where Ares is standing in front of Smoke, challenging him, and squeezes past Ares with her little body. Ares looks at her strangely and backs up as she takes a swing. It's like she's Harley fucking Quinn or something as she rails Smoke in the kneecap.

Smoke hits the floor in pain and screams again, landing on his now wrecked knee. Gemma doesn't waste time, swinging the bat around again like she's playing in the major leagues, and she whacks him right in the balls. Right in the place where he should get to have nothing because of the way he treated women and children and the way he's used his position.

The sickness for me doesn't end, and I know it's only a matter of time before I puke. But this is totally worth it to see. Smoke is being made to crawl on the floor like a bug.

CHAPTER EIGHTEEN

PAN

I'm speechless at what the hell it is that my sister just did. My tiny little redheaded sister grabbed a baseball bat from behind the bar, came over to this guy like three times her size, even bigger than me, and just whacked him in the kneecap and the balls, taking him to the ground.

Things have been really rough with Gemma trying to accept that Trix and I are really together. But this, more than anything, shows that she supports us, or at least Trix, no matter what she says or how angry she is. Trix told Gemma her story, something I know was hard, and Gemma came out swinging, literally.

I guess I've kind of underestimated my little sis. She can clearly take care of herself, even in this world.

Smoke gets up somehow after crawling past us like a cock-roach. He pulls himself up to the bar and begins slowly walking away. But Gemma is on his heels. She keeps going after him, this time getting him in the back of the head and in the neck. I'm surprised I don't hear a crunch, though I suppose she could only put so much force behind the thing.

I know I need to stop this before he recovers enough to do some shit, so I go up to Gemma and pull her off. I rip the bat out of her hands and throw it to the floor. "This isn't your fight, Gemma," I say it softly, so she knows she's not in trouble, and I do appreciate it. But I need to get her to stop. I can't have this guy after two women, and he's trying to get out of here. I'm not sure we can let that happen now.

She turns on me and glares. "It is, Pan. Trixie is just as much family to me as you are. Don't you get it now?"

I blink a few times, just staring at her. Now Smoke is clinging to the bar for support. She probably whacked him hard enough that he has a concussion as well as his obviously broken kneecap. He's trying to land himself in a seat and failing miserably.

I look down at Gemma, who clears her throat and begins to announce to the whole damn bar, "Congratulations, everyone, on sharing this damn bar with a sick bastard. He claims to be a priest, someone from the church, someone devoted to helping orphans, but instead, he tortures and rapes them."

I tap her on the shoulder, trying to get her to quit. I know the rest of his club is in here because I saw them when we got here. We don't need another enemy like the Vile Serpents, no matter how much I hate this one guy. But she doesn't stop. "This guy thinks that teenage girls are tempting, and he acts on it."

The rest of his MC comes up to us and looks at him. One of the other members asks, "Is what this chick is saying true, Smoke?" He looks almost nervous to find out the answer.

"I don't know who the hell any of those people are. They just don't like that I came up to one of their ol' ladies and told her she was pretty. I haven't done anything." His words come out robotically in between gasps as he tries to get ahold of himself. He's finally sitting on a chair now.

A man steps forward from the MC, and I see that he has the Prez patch. His name patch says, Ranger. "I'm not gonna fucking ask you again. Is what this girl says true? Are you some kind of sicko?"

This time, Smoke has the wherewithal to look frightened as he stares down his Prez. He nervously stutters, "I told you. I haven't done anything."

Ranger shakes his head and sighs, and I wonder what the hell is going to happen next. "You were always the worst at lying. Maybe it's the one thing that I can give you credit for as a priest." Ranger suddenly pulls out his gun and shoots Smoke right in the head. Smoke falls backward off the bar chair, bleeding onto the floor.

"Do you hear that?" Ranger asks, turning on the rest of his club. "It's bad enough if you've done shit like that in your past, but you need to own up to it. You need to pay for it. Don't ever fucking lie to me."

The manager comes out of the office, looking around to find out what the hell is going on. "What happened out here? You know this is neutral territory," he reminds us, looking like he might go grab his shotgun from the back. It wouldn't be the first time. It's almost like deja vu, considering he had to pull it out on Thorn more than once.

It's Gemma who speaks up to answer him. "There was a pedophile in your bar." He freezes, processing it.

"Don't worry, we'll clean it up. You should probably get ready to close up shop, though," I tell him to diffuse things.

"We'll help out," Ranger offers. A couple of stragglers from other MCs come up, offering to help and promising to keep it a secret so that the cops don't have to get involved. That's what's best to maintain neutral territory for the bar and best for everyone in all the clubs.

I want to relax and breathe a sigh of relief because everything is good. We've obliterated another threat. The problem is, I know it's not the last one still out there, and if it's not Thorn, it'll be something else. It's the MC life. There's always a threat coming up, and now I have to deal with that with Trix by my side. I have to protect her.

I walk up to her and see that she's definitely turned pale. Of course, she just watched somebody get killed right in front of her after confronting the person who did all those awful things to her. I offer to take her back to the club with me, and she doesn't fight. In fact, all the girls decide to come back with us. What a crazy fucking night.

When we get up to my room, I tuck her in bed real nice and kiss her on the head. "You'll never have to worry about him again," I whisper to her as she falls asleep.

It's not even starting to become light outside yet when I wake up to a tossing and turning Trixie.

Things have been weird since the incident at *Shots,* where we all watched Smoke's brains get blown out for his behavior. Trix has been at the clubhouse with me ever since, and she doesn't seem herself.

She's been sick ever since that gas station sushi, but honestly, it's been too damn long for her to be sick unless it's something more serious.

Or unless she isn't sick at all.

Either way, her restlessness worries me, so I get up and ride to the drugstore across the way for some essentials. She needs to get some food down, even if it's just a bowl of soup. I grab some lozenges, too, with ginger in them for her nausea. I hear they work pretty damn well.

The last thing I need to get scares me just a little. It's not that I wouldn't be incredibly happy, but I'm young and not the most perfect man. Either way, Trix and I need our answers.

I know for a fact that Trix hasn't been on the rag even once since we've been together. We haven't been apart long enough for that. Now, she could be on something that stops her period, but there's another possibility. Trix could be pregnant, which would explain her prolonged nausea and bad dreams without explanation.

I check my haul out with the sleepy clerk at the front and head back to my girl. If there's anyone I want a baby with, it's Trix. She'd make some damn beautiful babies. By her side, I'm sure I can learn to be a great dad.

By the time I get up the stairs in the clubhouse, I feel more at peace with the idea that she might be pregnant. I know we will handle it together, just like all the other shit we've done so far. We've got this.

CHAPTER NINETEEN

I wake up disappointed that I don't feel any better. I stretch and yawn, looking over at the empty bed next to me. I realize then that Pan has gone somewhere. Considering it's his room, I don't have too much to worry about, but when I feel like shit, I hate being lonely.

I've been staying with him at the clubhouse for the past two days. The incident at *Shots* really shook me, but on top of that, I'm still not feeling well. I'm beginning to think that it's not food poisoning, that it must be something else.

I promised Pan that if it doesn't get better by tomorrow, then I'm gonna go into an urgent care or something and see if it's stomach flu or something else. Maybe parasites. I mean, Alabama water is not exactly known for its cleanliness.

My stomach gurgles, but not in hunger. The last time I tried to eat it was half a bowl of cereal, and I threw most of it back up. The rest of it feels like it's just floating around in my stomach and not going anywhere. My digestion has gone to shit.

Then again, I'm aware from all the years of attempting to heal from my PTSD over my childhood that trauma can cause a lot of stomach issues. So, I could be reacting to seeing Smoke again and the way he tried to pull me into the bathroom.

That could have been so much worse. I owe a hell of a lot to the club, but even more to Gemma.

She came in to talk to me after we got back to the club that night. I was still puking my guts out at that point, but we both chalked it up to what I had just witnessed. I didn't know at that point if the image of Smoke dead on the floor of *Shots* was a positive or negative one, and it kind of felt like a part of me had died with him.

I'm ready to grow wings and transform now instead of spending my days in front of a toilet, worshipping the bowl.

I'm glad for what came out of it between Gemma and me, though. She apologized for the way she reacted to finding out that I was going to be together with her brother. She had made some assumptions about him based on his past behavior that he was going to hurt me, and since we were close and that was her brother, she thought it would make things different between her and me if he did.

I think she realizes now that Pan is serious about me, even if he's never been serious in the past. So, in a roundabout way, we have her blessing, though I don't think she'll ever say that out loud.

She went back to the house with Pearl, and Calli stayed the night that night too, but now Calli and Eros are back in the house too. I had to stay because I was too weak to get on the back of Pan's bike. I probably would have retched all over the road and caused a car accident or some shit.

The door of the room squeaks open, and in walks Pan carrying a grocery bag. I turn and look at the alarm clock and see that it's only a little bit after 5:00 a.m. So, for some reason, he's gone out to the store this early.

He sits down on the side of the bed next to me, and I notice the logo on the bag is from the 24-hour drugstore just across the road. He pulls something out, and I realize it's a bag of lozenges. Ginger.

"I'm so sorry you still feel bad. I figured you could use some things for it." Pan opens a lozenge for me and pops it into my mouth. It's so sweet and intimate that there's an ache in my center, but that ache leads to nausea. I start to gag as I try and get comfortable again on the bed until I begin sucking on the ginger. As it goes down and coats my throat and goes into my stomach, there's a little bit of soothing there. I should have thought of it sooner.

We sit there in silence as I suck on the soothing lozenge for a couple of minutes. When I'm feeling a little bit better, I try to sit up. "What's up? What else is in the bag," I ask him, leaning over and being nosy. That's when he pulls out a pregnancy test and pops it on my lap. I just stare down at it like he's just given me a dead rat or something as a gift.

"What the hell is this for?"

Pan rubs the back of his neck and then captures my eyes with his. "Look, I'm not an idiot. I know some people think I am, but I know how a woman's body works for the most part. Since we've been together, I've never seen you or heard of you going on the rag. You need to take this damn test and see if that's the reason you've been sick for so long."

I start doing the math in my head and realize how right he is. I've been under so much stress lately that I forgot. I think back to the first time that we had sex and the second time and remember that no protection was used. I'm on the shot, but I know plenty of women who get pregnant anyway. I guess I do need to take the test.

"Okay," I say, taking a deep breath to calm my nerves. The last thing I need right now is to puke all over the test. That would certainly be a fun reading.

I get up and go to the restroom, shutting the door. I double-check all the directions to make sure I'm doing it right and then pee on the stupid stick. I try to laugh at myself for doing this and promise that it'll be something to talk about later and joke about, that there's no way I'm pregnant. Then, I put the cap back on the test and head back into the room with Pan.

Despite the situation, he looks perfectly calm and collected. I don't know if it's a good sign or bad, but I do know I'm glad he's here.

I set the test on the nightstand and hold his hand. We wait for the five minutes together. It feels like ages. I hate the paradox of time in situations like this.

My phone goes off to let us know we've waited long enough, and I swear my knuckles turn white with how hard I'm squeezing Pan's hand. We both lean over the test at the same time, and my whole body drains of blood as I look at the positive result.

I'm pregnant.

We're pregnant.

I don't know whether I'm supposed to be happy or terrified, but I'm entirely shaking. I look up at Pan, wondering what the hell's going through his head, and can't believe I see a smirk on his face of all things.

"We'll handle this the same way we handle everything else, together," he tells me, pulling me in for a gentle kiss. I melt into it. "And in case you didn't already know, I love you, Trix."

I'm carrying Pan's baby, and he loves me. My body relaxes with his soothing voice and touch. I can trust him. I know we haven't been together the longest, but I can do this with him here. I'm secure enough in him to have this baby with him.

"I love you too. We're going to have a baby," I whisper to him and to myself, most importantly. "We're going to be parents."

He wraps his arm around me, kissing me as he pulls me down into the bed. We lay there like that for a while, just enjoying being in each other's arms.

CHAPTER TWENTY

PAN

I pull up to the building downtown and park my bike near the front. I get off the bike and turn around to help Trix off, being extra delicate with her. She keeps telling me that I'm babying her and being too paranoid, but she's carrying my baby, and she's been feeling like shit. It's the least I can do to make sure she and the baby are safe and cared for. I worry a little that the bike is shaking the baby around too much, which makes her laugh every time I bring it up.

Instinctively, I know that's not how it works, but it's an automatic reaction, especially after everything that's been going on in our lives. Trix and I have been through a lot together and separately. This baby is a beautiful thing and a miracle, and I'm going to treat it as such.

I hold her hand as we walk through the automatic doors and into the building. It's a small medical complex with several doctors in it, and we have to look at the directory near the stairs to find out exactly where we're supposed to go. It looks like we're meant to be on the third floor, so I lead her to the elevator. "I will not have you taking the stairs today."

"While it is fucking annoying that you baby me, I appreciate that. I don't think my stomach could handle going up the stairs like that right now. I'd probably throw up anything I've had today," Trix says.

I look at her for a moment, seeing that despite the fact that she feels so terrible, there's a glow about her. The female body is amazing. All the things they can go through and still handle everything, all while looking good doing it, it's crazy.

The elevator opens and makes that dinging sound when we get to the third floor. There aren't a lot of people around, seeing as we got the first appointment of the day. I want plenty of time to enjoy this and process what we're about to see.

It's Trix's first appointment with her obstetrician. I'm extremely proud of the fact and grateful that she's asked me to come. I know we agreed to do this together, but she has every right to turn me down when it comes to going to appointments like this. It's kind of private, what her body is going to be going through, and I don't want to pry if she feels uncomfortable.

At the front desk of the obstetrician's office, we have to fill out some paperwork. There are things like how far along she believes she is, if she's had previous pregnancies before, and just general health questions.

My leg starts bouncing with nervousness and anticipation, and Trix reaches over just as she finishes her forms to stop my leg from bouncing. "I'm the one who's pregnant, you know. You're going to give me a coronary if you don't chill out," she says, glaring at me.

I look back at her and force my leg to stop.

It's not too long before a nurse comes out to get us. We go back into a room where Trix recounts a lot of the things that she filled out on the paperwork. They offer her an STD panel, as well as a confirmation pregnancy test. She has to leave the room for a bit while they take her blood and a pee sample.

I really hope I find a way to chill the fuck out by the time the baby gets here because this is nerve-wracking as hell already. I can't imagine the way I'm going to be smothering and constantly scared for the well-being of Trix and our kid if I don't learn to breathe and cut this shit out. But it's one of the first good things I've ever done in my life. I've helped create this incredible life.

Trix comes back, and then the doctor comes in shortly after to talk to her. They go over several instructions on how to take care of herself during this time. She gives instructions on taking prenatal vitamins, exercises she can do, and ways to sleep to help herself feel more comfortable. Then, she luckily gets some nausea medicine as well. I think we're both relieved by that part.

The poor woman can't help but throw up almost everything she eats, and there hasn't been a single craving that has proved to be helpful against that. She still can't keep anything down despite the fact that I've made several runs for food in the middle of the night.

"If you don't mind, I'd like to have an ultrasound done to get an idea of exactly how far along you are since you're not sure. It's always good to have that baseline so that we can gauge the progress of the pregnancy and the growth of the baby to make sure everything is normal when you're coming in here. It also gives us a good idea of when you're going to be able to find out whether it's a girl or boy."

The doctor smiles as she explains all this to us, and I'm getting good vibes from her. I hope we'll form a good relationship so we can trust her to deliver this baby. Or at least so Trix can trust her since she's kind of necessary in that part of things.

I want my baby to have the best.

Trix agrees to the ultrasound, and I see her get excited. She's smiling as they're bringing the ultrasound machine in, and they are laying her back. It's kind of a weird process as they put this weird goo on her stomach. I've never been a part of any of this before and had no idea how this part works.

A small wand is sliding over Trix's exposed stomach now, and I can see inside her if I look at the machine. I hold her hand as I watch, both fascinated and weirded out. The human body sure does look strange. There's all this fluid floating around in there. All of a sudden, I spot this small dark circle on the screen. When it comes into view, there's an intense thumping.

"There's the baby's heartbeat," the nurse says happily, pointing to it on the screen and leaving it to sit there for minutes so we can listen to the rhythm.

Trix squeezes my hand, and I look at her. She's so happy. I've been a little bit worried that she's not as enthusiastic about this child as I am, but I can see it in her eyes now. That motherly instinct is already there, even though the baby's still not that big. "So, can you tell how far along I am?" Trix asks the woman as the ultrasound progresses.

"From experience, if I had to guess, I'd say the baby is measuring about 11 weeks or so. There's always a little bit of wiggle room because, of course, not every baby is the same size. It's a range, but I'd say we're average for that time period," she answers.

I start doing the mental math for that to add up and realize it has to be the first or second time we were together. So, this whole time a child has been growing inside her unbeknownst to us.

That very first explosive encounter between us, the amazing time we had, had already entwined our fates together without us even knowing. The universe must be having a good laugh right about now, and I guess I can laugh along with her.

We finish up the appointment, and Trixie goes to clean herself up from the goo being on her stomach from the ultrasound. Another appointment is scheduled for 20 weeks along, or approximately 20 weeks along, to double-check her progress as well as to tell us the sex of the baby.

As we walk out of the building, there's a better air about Trix already and prescriptions in hand for me to take to the pharmacy for her. I ask, "So, do you want it to be a boy or a girl?"

"I don't know. I kind of feel like it's a boy. But I love it either way." I nod along, wondering if her intuition is going to be right about that.

I get on the bike and dare to ask, "Are you hungry? I can go fill these prescriptions real quick, and you can have your nausea meds, and I can take you out for lunch."

"As long as it's not sushi," she comments with a little laugh. Now I know she's feeling better. A lot of what's been going on with her must have been nerves.

"Ha fucking ha." I laugh sarcastically at her. Of course, she brings up the damn sushi.

Trix giggles at me and then pulls one of the ginger lozenges out of my jacket pocket and pops it into her mouth to keep from gagging and puking on the damn road while we ride.

It's kind of hot that she just reached into my pocket like that, but I doubt that fucking is on her mind at all right now. Though she keeps promising me she's in all these mommy forums now, and they talk about how the second trimester is much better, and in fact, all the women fuck like rabbits.

I have to admit, I'm looking forward to that, but I can't blame her for how she feels now. I've been doing a little research myself, so I can understand what she's going through and all the changes her body has to deal with, and all the hormones are enough to make me sick just thinking about it.

Not to mention the discomfort and pain. Her body has to change to accommodate a whole other fucking person.

Crazy.

After a quick stop at the pharmacy, where I get them to fill her prescriptions right then and there, I grab a bottle of water for her to down her prenatal and anti-nausea medication with, and then we're off to an early lunch.

I try to think about what she might be able to eat. I didn't want to overwhelm her stomach, but I couldn't believe the list of things the doctor had told her weren't necessarily safe for the baby. Sushi or anything undercooked . . . she can't even eat lunch meat because she might catch listeria.

I end up opting for a little Italian joint. Not a chain but a small, family-owned place where the food is cooked slowly and to perfection. There's ambiance music playing softly as we walk in and take any seats we want since it's not lunch rush yet. In fact, the sign tells me they just opened not too long ago.

"This place looks yummy," Trix says as she is handed a menu by the waiter and then asks for lemon water. I think she's getting sick of all the ginger ale.

Both of us end up getting soup, salad, and breadsticks. It's simple, and it's a bottomless thing, so I can eat however much I want or don't want. Trix seems to be favoring the soup—a Zuppa Toscana that she keeps moaning about every time she takes a bite.

"I'm guessing that the medication is working, then?" I ask her with a grin. She's so damn cute right now.

"I think so, but I probably need to slow down," she tells me. "I could just be taking it for granted. But food is so damn good right now. I've missed it."

I laugh at her and reach over the table to get a little string of parmesan off her lip that's stuck there. "I love you. You're so sexy and adorable at the same damn time," I tell her, looking her over.

Her cheeks flush bright red as she realizes how much I'm studying her. She puts her spoon down and looks away. "You don't have to be so shy about it. I look at you because you're beautiful."

"I know," she admits. "And I love you too. I just feel self-conscious right now. I mean, I'm bloated and feel big, despite the fact I'm not really eating."

"It's okay." I reach over and place my hand on top of hers, so she knows I mean it. "It's just the hormones talking. It's normal."

"Well, aren't you the expert," she teases, starting to eat again more slowly this time.

"Well, I figure if you're going to be having my baby for me and do all the hard work, I might as well at least know what you're going through." She looks up at me through hooded eyes, and my pants strain around my cock. Damn, she's amazing.

"So," I ask her as we get back on the bike, "do you want me to take you home or to the clubhouse?"

"Honestly, I'd rather stay with you for now," she says.

"Fine with me, of course. But I bet you're just using me for the foot massages and food I'm willing to get you in the middle of the night," I tease her.

"Maybe you're onto something." She winks

"When did you want to tell everyone?" I ask her before starting the engine. If I'm being honest, I'm a little excited to let everyone know we're having a baby. I want to shout it from the rooftops, but it's not really my decision.

"Well, I told you I just wanted to have the ultrasound first. I'm not quite 12 weeks yet, but I think it's okay now. Maybe we can text the girls to come over once we get to the club-house?" she asks.

"Of course, sounds like a plan." I rev the engine and take off, maybe a little too fast, but Trix's squeal is one of encourage-ment and happiness, not fear, as I go a little above the speed limit down the road. I can't wait to tell everyone the good news. I'm sure I'll be razzed for all this, but it's so damn worth it anyway.

We get to the club, and I immediately spot some trouble. Well, less trouble and more like drama. Zeus is walking around the lot, a woman shouting at him. I squint at her and recognize her as Calli's mother.

Not this again.

"You need to leave," Zeus tells her gruffly, pulling out a cigarette to smoke it. He leans against one of the bikes and tries to play calm and collected, but I can tell it's only surface level.

I also don't get why he's telling her to leave. Even though the woman seems kind of off and angry, even from Calli's own descriptions of her, as far as I know, Zeus still greatly cares for her. He left her and Calli behind because of a threat against them, that's it. The two of them definitely have some shit to work out.

I give Zeus a look and then lead Trix inside the clubhouse. It's the Prez's own business. Before we get to the door, we hear Calli's mom shout, "We're still married! I have a right to be here!"

"It's not my choice, woman. You won't sign the damn divorce papers!" Zeus hollers back with the cigarette hanging from his lips.

I know Calli's mom is Muslim and figure that must be why she hasn't. And poor Zeus is over here still caring about her while neither of them thinks they can work anything out.

I shake my head, hoping the two of them will get their heads out of their asses at some point and figure it out.

Walking through the door, Ares sees us and comes up to us. "Hey, you two, how's it going?" he asks. He's in a good mood, so I scan the place for Calli. Sure enough, she's already there, shooting the shit with Eros and Hermes on the couches.

"Well, we actually have something to tell everyone. I kinda want Gemma to be here first, though." Calli gets up and comes over to us with Eros' arm wrapped around her.

"What's going on with you two? You're not getting married, are you?" she asks, looking for a ring on Trix's finger.

I laugh. "No, I have not popped that question yet, but it is kind of big."

"I'll text Pearl," Calli offers.

Trix gets on the phone with Gemma to ask her to be there, but I don't know how long I can hold it in. It's killing me.

"They're on the way," Trix says. "She's getting Pearl in the truck now."

I nod. "I don't know how you do it. Keep this a secret," I whisper to her, getting looks from both Calli and Ares as they try to figure out what it is.

Gemma must have been speeding to get over here because she makes it from her house to the club in record time.

"Okay, what the fuck is all this about?" she asks me, smacking me on the shoulder.

"Well," I look at Trix, and she nods, "we're going to have a baby!"

Screams, cheers, noogies, squeals, and hugs commence from all sides. The overwhelming joy just reaffirms that this is my family, and I can't wait for my pride and joy to meet them all.

EPILOGUE

TRIX

6 months later . . .

I'm pacing the living room floor, and I'm pretty sure that I'm annoying the fuck out of everyone around me. For the past 24 hours, I haven't felt very well. While the second trimester went smoothly, just like everyone told me it would, the third trimester hit me differently. The fatigue was followed by days of feeling like I couldn't sleep. It's like a roller coaster. I've sometimes found myself awake for 48 hours straight, getting a bunch of baking done, and then I'll crash for almost an entire day.

All of the mommy blogs call the behavior nesting. It's these surges of energy that are supposed to help me get ready for all the things that we need when the baby comes. So, I've been given the bedroom with Gemma to myself now so that we have been able to put a crib in there and everything. Calli and Eros even went as far as to buy this really nice glider for us to have in there. The whole room is decked out in safari animals, and it's adorable.

Gemma and Calli share a room now, which works because Calli isn't always here, so Gemma still gets her privacy. I still spend a fair amount of time at the clubhouse, and there will be lots of people around there to help with the baby when it comes.

Some of the ol' ladies chipped in and got us a bassinet that is now sitting in Pan's room at the clubhouse too. For the first couple of months, the baby will be here before making the transition into a crib.

There's something about today, though. This energy I have is restless energy. I can't seem to get anything specific done, and I try to chalk it up to the fact that I'm nervous about Pan. He is out of state and out of reach, on a run for the club.

Apparently, the night that he had to leave me alone was because there was some kind of suspicious vehicle they were looking into. When they got the plates' information back, they figured out that the plates belonged to Tennessee. So, in the middle of the summer, they decided to get their bikes and take a run to visit the Skulls Renegade MC to see if they might know something about it. And if not, they could at least keep a lookout for this vehicle, whatever it is and whoever it belongs to.

I don't exactly feel nauseous, but I'm in a lot of pain, more pain than I've been in a while. The Braxton Hicks contractions are killing me, and walking seems to be the best thing to soothe them at the moment. At least it keeps my brain occupied.

I haven't heard from Pan in 24 hours now, and it worries me what the hell he might be getting himself into. I keep thinking about the injury that I had to stitch up months ago and how he could get another one that's just as bad or worse.

I don't even wanna think about how many candles I've lit for him. It's ridiculous, and Gemma has made fun of me for it more than once.

She's learned very quickly not to laugh at a pregnant woman. It does not bode well for anyone.

I didn't like the way Pan and I left it either. Not that we're on the rocks or anything, but we did have a fight about him going. And again, he was telling me how I don't understand how he has to do whatever the Prez says. The MC is like his job, and Zeus is his boss.

But it's more than that. It's a little bit closer to a slave contract if you ask me. I know a lot of it's the hormones talking. I'm angry, and I'm fearful. I don't like when he's not here. But also, I'm huge. I'm 35 weeks pregnant and entirely uncomfortable. It's more than just a minor inconvenience that Pan isn't here.

I also, in a few days, start a weekly checkup with the obstetrician to check my progress because technically, while I'm not due until week 40, she warned me that I can go into labor at any point past 36 weeks. And that if I show signs of any problems or the baby does, they'll have to induce.

Not that we think there's going to be anything unhealthy because I've been pretty healthy the whole damn time, but there is always the possibility of bumps in the road. I told him he has to be back for that. In fact, I got in Zeus' face before they all left to let him know that Pan better come back in one piece before that first weekly appointment.

Calli and Eros actually thought it was funny to see a bare-foot, pregnant lady yelling at Zeus. It's probably something I'll find funny as hell later on, but I'm not laughing now.

"Do you have to Braxton Hicks!?" I say loudly as another wave hits. This time it's really intense, and I have to pause my walking. I wrap my hands around my abdomen and push at my lower spine as a contraction squeezes my entire pelvic area.

"Are you sure that those aren't real contractions, honey?" Calli's mother asks in a thick accent. She's been staying here for a few days.

She keeps coming back, not just to see Calli, but I think to figure out what the hell is going to happen between her and Zeus. They fight a lot, but they never come to a resolution. Apparently, there's been divorce papers sent to her several times, but she won't sign them. Something about her religion. But she seems to be more likely to cooperate if he'll just talk to her first. She wants answers about some things that she's had a lot of time to think about.

I think Calli kind of hopes that the two of them will work it out, but I don't know after that many years apart and that much hurt that it's possible. It might just be best for a clean break. Only time will tell.

"They can't possibly be real contractions. I mean, I'm only 35 weeks and three days."

As if on cue, the universe decides to laugh down at me as my water breaks all over the floor. "Oh my God, Oh my God." I can't be going into labor right now. Not at 35 weeks, and certainly not with Pan not here. This is ridiculous.

"It's okay. Just breathe." Calli's mom gets up and comes over to me, taking my hand and walking me toward the couch to sit down. "Labor happens at different times, but usually, it takes a while. Even when the water breaks. The best thing for you to do right now is to keep calm," she explains.

I take some deep breaths and close my eyes, trying to get to that zen place. It's kind of hard to find right now, considering the situation, but I commit. "Okay, what now? Is my baby going to be okay? I mean, I'm only 35 weeks."

Calli's mother kneels down in front of me. In the meantime, she also motions to Calli. "Callista, go make the car comfortable for your friend here. We will be taking her to the hospital shortly, but I'm going to get her calm and see how far apart the contractions are."

Calli springs into action, immediately grabbing her keys and some pillows, and goes out to her car. Her mother turns to me and begins to explain what I'm going to be experiencing next. "You're going to start having contractions. As your cervix opens, they will become more intense. But it's a good sign that they still feel like Braxton Hicks to you because it means that they're not very strong yet, and you're not that close to giving birth. We have time."

She leads me through several more calming breaths before she continues to explain. Another contraction hits, and I find myself squeezing the fabric of the couch to pull through it. Now that I think about it, today, it has been more intense than the typical Braxton Hicks. I guess these are real. But she's right. It's nothing I can't breathe through. Just an inconvenience right now.

"Okay, good job. You're going to be fine. You'll get through this. At 35 weeks, the baby should be fine. There may be a couple of things like watching for jaundice or learning how to feed, but it should be fine. Nothing major is left to develop at this point."

I'm glad I have someone with experience with children to tell me these things and reassure me. Otherwise, I'd be freaking out and probably making it so much worse for myself.

Calli comes back into the house and helps me get dressed into something that I'm going to be comfortable in. I'd like to keep the gown at the hospital off for as long as possible. I have a nice summer dress that I put on, and I slip on some shoes before both women help me out to the car and get me down into the passenger seat.

I'm handed my phone and directed to go ahead and text Pan, though I know he most likely won't be responding. He warned me that sometimes up in the mountains like that, the signal is not so great and that he would probably not be allowed to answer unless it was an emergency.

"He's not going to answer," I tell Calli.

"It's okay. I'll call my dad," she says, hooking up her phone to the Bluetooth of the car as she starts driving us to the hospital. "I'll call him and then Gemma, okay?" All I can seem to do is nod and furrow my brows.

I don't like this shit at all. I know I won't be alone in this. I'll have my girls at my side, but I want Pan.

"What is it, Calli?" Zeus answers the phone, and I feel at least some relief knowing he had the wherewithal to pick up the damn phone.

"We need you to send Pan home. Trix is going into labor. I'm taking her to the hospital now."

"Shit. Even going fast, he's a good five or six hours away."

"I just went into labor. He can make it," I tell him over the Bluetooth.

"Okay, I'll send him off. Take care of her for us."

"We will, and Mom's here to help."

"At least there's that." Zeus hangs up, and I feel a little bit better about the idea. Pan will be here in time to do this with me. It's a mantra I say in my head even as I go through the exams and they tell me I'm already 6 cm.

I keep telling myself when they give me the epidural and put all of the monitoring on the baby and me, the contractions kick up to an unworldly intensity, shooting me straight into 8 cm and nearly fully effaced.

"I'm sorry, honey, but it looks like this is going fast. You'll probably be pushing within the hour," Callista's mother tells me with a sad look. I've only been here for two hours. It means Pan won't be here until this is all said and done, even if he's speeding like a hellcat down the highway.

I'm about to panic when Gemma comes rushing into the room. "I'm here, I'm here!" she screams, immediately pulling up a chair to my bedside. "I had to beg to leave work early, but I won't be missing this. What's the status?"

"I'm going to be doing this without him," I say with tears in my eyes. "The baby is coming fast."

"That's okay. Auntie Gemma is here for both of you." She taps my stomach and smiles, and I'm so damn grateful she's been over her shit for months now. She's the only other person I could do this with.

Shortly thereafter, I am wracked with a huge contraction and pressure telling me to push. It's chaos as Calli and her mother are whisked out to the waiting room, Gemma squeezing my hand while the nurse and doctor come in ready to deliver the baby. The whole thing is a blur as I am told when and how to push. Luckily, the epidural makes me numb enough that I'm not crying out in pain, but it's exhausting as fuck as I push this baby out of me.

When I'm done, a beautiful baby boy is held up for all to see as he screams and wiggles.

"He looks so healthy. He'll be fine, Momma," the nurse tells me, wrapping him in a blanket and laying him on my chest.

"Hi, little Atlas," I say as I begin to cry.

Several hours later, Atlas is resting while Gemma watches, and Pan finally shows up. I've been told to get some sleep, but I've been trying to pump instead to get my supply up for him. He does have a bit of a sucking delay, and they said the more healthy supply I have, the more that would help him. Plus, I can't sleep without seeing Pan.

There are tears in his eyes when he enters the room. "Fuck, Trix, I never should have gone." He rushes to me and holds me to him carefully while we both cry from emotional exhaustion.

"I feel like such an ass. How is he?" he asks, pulling away.

"Shhh," Gemma says, "He's sleeping. Come see." Pan walks over and looks down at our son, and I see him swell with pride.

"You should know the whole damn club practically is in the waiting room. They all came back with me."

I laugh for the first time, understanding what this whole MC thing is all about—it's family. "Did you bring the hospital bag with you?" he asks, turning around.

"Um . . . what the hell is that? I didn't even think about that shit. I was only 35 weeks." We both laugh because neither of us knows what we're doing, but I know we'll figure it out together.

If you're not already following me, check me out on the following!

Facebook
Facebook Reader's Group
Goodreads
Bookbub
Amazon
Instagram
Tiktok